Sweet Dreams BOUTIQUE

A DEBUT NOVEL

THERE'S NOTHING SWEET ABOUT IT

J.F. SIMS

Copyright © 2022 by JF Sims Publishing

All rights reserved. No part of this publication may be reproduced, distributed, or transmitted in any form or by any means, including photocopying, recording, electronic, mechanical, or other means without the express written consent of the publisher.

This is a work of fiction. Names, characters, places, and incidents are the product of the writer's imagination or are used fictitiously, and any resemblance to any actual persons, living or dead, events, or locales is purely coincidental. If you would like permission to use material from the book, please email the author: j.f.sims@j.f.sims.com.

CONTENTS

Acknowledgments v
Dedication vii
Prologue ix

Chapter 1 Bad Company 1
Chapter 2 All That Glitters 10
Chapter 3 The Devil's Nectar 19
Chapter 4 A Serious Matter 27
Chapter 5 Where There's Smoke 36
Chapter 6 These Three Words 42
Chapter 7 The Devil's Playground 50
Chapter 8 The Enemy's Snare 56
Chapter 9 The Sweetness of Wine 63
Chapter 10 A Long Time Coming 69
Chapter 11 Lord, Guide my Tongue 75
Chapter 12 No Other Way 82
Chapter 13 Dishonor 88
Chapter 14 All Manner of Lies 96
Chapter 15 Near the Cross 104

Chapter 16 Hold on to Hope 111
Chapter 17 The Storm is Coming... 119
Chapter 18 Deliver Me from Evil... 127
Chapter 19 Surrender.. 134
Chapter 20 Opened Door..141
Chapter 21 Ain't Nothing Free... 150
Chapter 22 The Naked Truth... 156
Chapter 23 The Assignment..161
Chapter 24 A Path to Victory... 167
Chapter 25 A Small Win..173
Chapter 26 Clean Hands..179
Chapter 27 Committed Sacrifice.. 186
Chapter 28 All Rise.. 192
Chapter 29 Unhinged.. 197
Chapter 30 The Final Say.. 204
Chapter 31 Deliverance... 212

Epilogue 216

ACKNOWLEDGMENTS

All glory belongs to God, and I give Him thanks for gifting me with the ability to put pen to paper and create a work of this magnitude. He is, has always been, and will continue to be my guiding force and I pray this novel brings Him honor.

I am blessed to be surrounded by so many people who walked with me on this journey. First, I thank my husband - Larry, my children: Crystal, LaJoi, Trey, and Nicholas, and my grandchildren: Cailyn, Carson, and Caleb, for your unwavering love and support. Thank you for lifting me when I fall, believing when I doubt and making this life worth living.

To my extended family and friends (of which there are too many to name) who helped shape who I am today, I thank God for each of you and I pray continued blessings upon you.

I am eternally grateful for my literary consultant, Norma L. Jarrett, who has not hesitated to offer me her guidance and expertise. To my copy editor, Candice "Ordered Steps" Johnson (Bingeworthy Books), you gave this book wings, and I will forever be indebted to you.

To my Beta Readers and Launch Team–LaToya Barnett, LaJoi

Boone, Kayeaka Bracken, Lakesia Butler, Michaela Cotner, Carolyn Flynn, Geoffrey Lofton, Lyvetta Marshall, Joya Sigee, Crystal Sims, Morgan Toomer, and Christina Warner, many, many thanks for your feedback, encouragement, and book promotion. You are the dream team! Much love, always.

And finally, this book is written in memory of the late Dorothy Vinson—thank you for always being a light, giving me hope, and showing me love. You were the first to make this possible.

DEDICATION

Sweet Dreams Boutique is dedicated to my loving husband and biggest cheerleader–Pastor Larry B. Sims Jr. Without your persistent nudging and unyielding support, this novel would be nothing more than a passing thought in the recesses of my mind. I love you beyond measure. Thank you for believing books were inside me, and for always having my back. The best is still yet to come!

PROLOGUE

Summer 1998

"You shouldn't have to *beg* for anything when you have a money-maker between your thighs," LaShaun heard as she lay in bed eavesdropping on Sadie, her next-door neighbor.

Sadie ran an illegal beauty salon during the day and a gambling operation at night. Her kitchen window was parallel to LaShaun's bedroom window, and only four feet separated the two. So, when both were hoisted to let in the occasional breeze, LaShaun overhead things fourteen-year-old girls should never know.

"I'd rather die than sell my body to the highest bidder," a female declared disdainfully. LaShaun wasn't sure, but she believed her to be Ms. Dora-the organist, choir director, and soloist at Gateway Baptist Church. Ever the curious one, LaShaun was compelled to verify.

Knowing Sadie's keen ears would hear the bed creak if she moved too quickly, LaShaun sneakily eased onto her knees and inched closer to the wall. Then, she pressed the tip of her nose against it and slid to her left, toward the window.

When she got close to the opening, she moved her head slightly to the left and caught a glimpse of Sadie standing behind a chair. Her left hand was palm up, and long strands of kinky hair lay over it. Her right hand held a straightening comb, and she slowly moved it down the thick strands, careful not to burn herself.

Her five feet eight frame and wide curvy hips blocked LaShaun's view of her client. However, the length of the person's hair told LaShaun it couldn't be Dora. For Dora's hair had fallen out when she tried to give herself a silky perm. Now, it was no longer than a pinky finger.

"Who is that?" LaShaun whispered before she sucked her teeth in frustration. The sound made Sadie's head swivel to the right, and LaShaun instinctively jerked her head backward. She held her breath to be extra quiet. When Sadie continued her conversation, LaShaun exhaled. Then, just as she grew bored with their banter, Sadie scolded the person talking and added, "Stop complaining to me, then! You can *stay* in the dark for all I care!"

LaShaun cupped her hands over her mouth and snickered. *I knew she was talking to Dora.*

The electric company disconnected Dora's power regularly and Lucille- LaShaun's foster mother and the bookkeeper at Gateway Baptist Church, often complained about her draining the church's benevolence fund.

Before LaShaun could get off her knees and lay down again, she felt the sting of the belt travel across her back. Instantaneously, she screamed and hunched her back inward as she turned her upper torso towards her assailant.

Unfortunately, the move caused Lucille to strike her face accidentally. LaShaun yelped in agony as she grabbed the nearest pillow to cover herself. Lucille was sixty years old but had the strength of an ox. She easily yanked the pillow from her and flung it to the floor.

Trapped like an animal, LaShaun cowered to the corner of her bed and raised her knees to her chest. At five feet one and only one hundred and five pounds, her thin frame twisted and contorted as the belt hit her thighs, arms, and back. With each lash, Lucille chanted, "Didn't. I. Tell. You. About. Eavesdropping."

Tears streamed down LaShaun's face like a waterfall as she howled, "I'm sorry. I won't do it again!" But Lucille didn't relent. So, as the belt continued to connect with her skin, LaShaun bellowed in anguish and shielded her head as best she could.

Sadie hollered at Lucille from her window, commanding her to stop hitting LaShaun, but it didn't matter. Lucille ignored her until her whipping arm grew tired, and she couldn't raise it anymore. LaShaun didn't get relief until Lucille stood, huffing and puffing, trying to catch her breath.

Finally, when Lucille's labored breathing slowed to a manageable pace, she squinted her eyes, gritted her teeth, and ordered, "Close that window and get your fast behind in the living room. Ain't nothing over there but misery and trouble."

LaShaun sniffled and wiped her eyes as she begrudgingly obeyed.

Whilst the window was open, Sadie threatened, "You beat her like that again, and you'll answer to me!"

"Keep running your mouth, and you'll answer to the police," Lucille bellowed angrily. "Mind your business and stay out of mine."

"She is my business," Sadie admonished. "If you don't want her, send her to me." Lucille snorted and walked out of the room.

LaShaun would give anything to stay with Sadie. Even though Lucille criticized her for being a "woman of ill-repute," LaShaun adored her. Sure, she broke a few laws to make ends meet, but she didn't have a choice. "In a man's world, a woman's gotta do what a woman gotta do," she'd heard Sadie say often. And LaShaun took her at her word.

Despite the summer's scorching temperatures, Lucille forbade LaShaun from opening her window or playing with her friends for the rest of the summer. She wasn't allowed to sit on the front porch unless Lucille accompanied her.

When Sadie sat on her porch and tried to hold a conversation, Lucille ignored her. To stay out of trouble, LaShaun did the same. So, for two weeks, she waited for school to arrive and dreamt of being anywhere but Lucille's home.

On the last day of summer break, Sadie followed LaShaun into a local shoe store. She stood by the door and watched as LaShaun handed the salesman a white sneaker with three black stripes down the side. When he went to the back of the store to retrieve the right size, Sadie walked over to her.

She tapped LaShaun's back. "Did you find what you want, baby girl?"

LaShaun's stomach fluttered when she heard the familiar voice, and she smiled. She didn't know whether Lucille could see her from the car, so she kept her back turned and answered, "Yes."

"It's okay to look at me when you speak...I'll handle Lucille," Sadie said sweetly.

Reluctantly, LaShaun slowly turned around. When she did, the salesman returned. He handed LaShaun the shoebox, and Sadie moved aside so LaShaun could go to a nearby bench to try them on. Sadie followed and sat next to her.

While she was bending to tie her laces, Sadie spoke. "Listen, baby girl," she began. "I know you're only behaving how you've seen Lucille behave toward me. But don't allow her to taint your spirit. She's old and being cantankerous is the only way she knows how to be. But you still have a lot of living ahead of you. So don't waste precious time being unkind and unloving. You're so much better than that."

LaShaun continued to look down as a big lump formed in her throat and her eyes watered. She blinked rapidly to keep the tears from falling, but one betrayed her emotions anyway. She wiped the tear away with the back of her hand, and Sadie rubbed her back. She always loved when Sadie showed her affection. For, unfortunately, it was the only time she received any.

After a few minutes passed, Sadie asked if she was okay. She cleared her throat and croaked, "Yes, Ma'am."

"Good," Sadie said lovingly. "Let's get these shoes rung up so you can get out of here. You're going to be the best-dressed girl in school."

LaShaun nodded in agreement and followed her to the register. She knew from times past that Sadie would pay for the shoes on her behalf, so she stood behind her and waited. When Sadie completed the transaction, she turned and handed LaShaun the bag.

LaShaun took it and hugged Sadie around her waist. "I'm sorry I was mean to you." She took a step backward.

"No need to be sorry. Just don't let anyone dictate your actions, but you," Sadie admonished.

LaShaun looked down without answering. Sadie used her right thumb and pointer to lift her head. "And there's nothing you can do to make me stop loving you."

LaShaun smiled brightly, gave her another hug, and left the store lighter and freer.

Later that night, her sleep was interrupted by the sound of rapid gunfire. Bad habits die hard, so she peeked out the window to see what was happening. She could hear people yelling and running but couldn't see clearly. Then, remembering the streetlights illuminated the front of her house, she ran to the living room.

As she opened her front door, someone screamed, "Call 9-1-1! Sadie's shot!" Her stomach dropped, she momentarily lost her breath, and a lump formed in her throat. Feeling she would vomit, she turned and sprinted to the bathroom. Lucille was standing in the hallway and was knocked against the wall.

Luckily, she was able to keep from falling. "You gon' mess around and get yourself shot trying to chase a bullet," Lucille snarled as she regained her balance. "Don't open my door no more!" LaShaun barely heard as she bent over the toilet, dry heaving.

Lucille waited by the door. "Breathe slowly. It'll pass in a minute."

When it did, LaShaun sobbed uncontrollably. Then, fearing the worst, she put her hands in a praying position as she pleaded, "God, let her be okay. Pleeeease."

Lucille watched quietly. And when LaShaun's crying stopped, she led her to the bedroom. LaShaun didn't think she could sleep but didn't voice it. She had no choice but to lay in her bed and listen to the sirens, wondering whether Sadie was still living or had died. Lucille promised to let her know as soon as she received news of her condition. She dozed off long after first-responders left the scene.

The alarm clock awakened her at seven-thirty, as it does every Sunday morning. When her eyes flittered open, they felt like somebody had thrown sand in them. Lying there, she prayed that everything was a bad dream. But, deep down, she knew better.

The smell of bacon told her Lucille was in the kitchen. Hearing mumbled voices, she got out of bed and grabbed her robe. As she got close enough to make out the voices, Dora was recounting last night's details. Then the phone rang.

"Yes, she's my daughter," Lucille said to the person on the other end of the line. LaShaun tiptoed so no one would hear her approach. "I will," she continued. "I'll be there as soon as possible." She gently placed the phone on the hook.

LaShaun entered the kitchen as Lucille looked at Dora and asked, "How do I tell LaShaun her momma just died?"

Chapter One
BAD COMPANY

December 2019

Growing up, LaShaun Delaney would lay in her bed with the windows open to hear Sadie Montgomery-her next-door neighbor, pour wisdom into the customers who paid her for a press and curl. And while her friends played hopscotch and jumped rope, LaShaun had a front-row seat to scandalous gossip and Sadie's worldview.

She wasn't raised in Sadie's home, hadn't eaten at her table, and hadn't been in her presence for long periods. But Sadie shaped LaShaun's mindset far more than Lucille-her sixty-year-old God-fearing foster mother, ever could. And what Sadie didn't teach her before she died, *Toni Morrison* and *Terri McMillan* did after.

As she cruised down I-20 from Atlanta towards Augusta- her hometown, she thought about Sadie and wondered whether she'd approve of her current lifestyle. She's now the first lady of Delaney Ministries International, a 7,000-member megachurch founded by her husband, Langston.

In less than an hour, she'll stand before twelve hundred women as the keynote speaker for the Women of Worth Conference at Greater New Zion Everlasting Christian Church.

Twelve years ago, when Langston told her he was starting his ministry, she'd wanted no parts of church life and had vehemently protested.

"I told you... I'm not a Christian, and I don't want to attend church every time the doors open," she'd argued.

"Once a Christian, always a Christian," he'd rebutted. Then, hugging her from behind and beaming like a Cheshire cat, he added, "When you placed your hand in God's hand and accepted Him as your Lord and Savior, you became a Christian...and you can't wash it off or wish it off!"

But Langston had no idea LaShaun never put her hands in God's hands, and she'd stopped believing in Him in the summer of 1998. That's when she'd accidentally learned Sadie was her biological mother, and Lucille-the woman she thought was her foster mother, was, in reality, her grandmother.

Lucille justified hiding the truth from her by quoting First Corinthians 15:33, "Bad company corrupts good morals." And, believing adults didn't answer to children, she'd offered no other explanation. So, LaShaun vowed never to forgive *her* for lying and keeping her mom's identity a secret-or God for allowing it to happen.

She'd learned the truth twenty-one years ago, but as LaShaun neared Augusta, she remembered that day vividly and the pain was just as real. She was lying in bed waiting for the alarm on her nightstand to go off. When it sounded, she rose from the bed in her Mulan t-shirt and pajama shorts and put on the pink plush bathrobe Sadie had gotten her for Christmas.

Sadie had been rushed to the hospital the night before with a gunshot wound, and LaShaun wanted an update. As she slowly walked towards the kitchen, she overheard the question that would haunt her forever.

"How am I going to tell LaShaun her momma just died?"

Overhearing Lucille, LaShaun let out a loud guttural wail and dropped to her knees in anguish. Then, like a mother who's told her only child has died, LaShaun doubled over and bellowed, "Noooo, she can't be dead, God. Pleeease...she can't be dead."

She cried long and uncontrollably before finding the strength to straighten her back and look at Lucille like a wounded pup. Lucille coaxed her to get up from the floor, but LaShaun felt too weak to obey. Finally, wiping her eyes, she begged in a faint childlike voice, "Please, tell me she's not dead. I don't want her to be dead."

Lucille, her own eyes wet with tears, remarked hoarsely, "I don't want her to be dead either, but it's too late now."

LaShaun's heart broke again. "Is she my mother?"

But she wasn't seeking an answer; she already knew the answer. And it explained Lucille and Sadie's love-hate relationship, the joy in LaShaun's heart when she was in Sadie's presence, and the fear in Lucille's eyes when Lashaun gushed over Sadie's beautiful caramel skin and long, naturally curly bohemian locs.

When Lucille didn't answer, LaShaun became filled with rage. At that moment, she realized Lucille's self-righteousness and deceit had kept her from experiencing the depth of her mother's love. Now, she'd never know the feeling of her *mother's* arms swaddling her when she was sad or embracing her after she'd reached a goal. And she'd never get the opportunity to say, "I love you," or experience the warmth blooming within when she heard, "I love you, more," in return.

She peered at Lucille with tears streaming down her face, rocking back and forth to calm the fury gradually boiling within her. Unwavering, Lucille lowered herself onto the old wooden two-post chair at the kitchen table.

She put her right elbow on the table and her fist to her mouth as she moaned, "*Umph, Umph, Umph,*" as if it were a magic chant that would make it all go away. LaShaun considered maybe she, too, understood the magnitude of what she'd done.

Only then did LaShaun feel Dora's hand softly rubbing the crown of her head. It was the only genuine affection she'd receive for years to come.

As she steered her cherry-red Tesla Roadster from I-20 onto the off-ramp leading to Washington Road, LaShaun's daydream was interrupted by her phone playing the gospel melody "*Deliver Me*," sung by LeAndria Johnson. Charlotte Montgomery-her best friend and business partner was trying to reach her via FaceTime.

LaShaun wiped tears from her eyes as she answered. Charlotte's pale white face appeared on her car's screen. She was wearing a black headband and white tank top, walking briskly through her neighborhood.

"Hey Charlotte, what's up?" She put on her blinkers and checked the left lane for cars. Thinking the lane was clear, she veered over.

Out of nowhere, a small black convertible zipped from her rear and entered the same lane, traveling well over the speed limit.

LaShaun slammed on the brakes to avoid a collision and laid on the horn as she hollered, "Idiot...learn how to drive!" She could hear Charlotte laughing as the teenage driver zoomed up the road pointing his middle finger towards the sky.

"Calm down, girl! You there yet?" Charlotte panted heavily.

Visibly annoyed, LaShaun gripped the steering wheel tightly. "I'll be there in ten minutes if these country bumpkins don't kill me first!"

Charlotte nodded. "You're making good time. You ready?"

LaShaun released a deep breath. Then she reached over to her bag to grab a tube of lipstick with her right hand as she steered with her left one. "Yes. I've given this message before, so it's no big deal."

"Since when did speaking to a thousand women become no big deal?" Charlotte stopped walking and briefly stretched at the edge of her driveway.

LaShaun put on lipstick. "You would have no trouble speaking either if the price was right."

"You're right about that." Charlotte walked from her driveway to the front door. LaShaun waited for her to take the key from the zippered pocket on her headband and unlock the door.

"I'll never understand why you don't go through the garage," LaShaun said as she shook her head in observation.

Charlotte ignored her. She entered her home, threw her keys on the console in the foyer, and kicked off her shoes. Then, she went to the kitchen, grabbed a bottle of water, and chugged it before continuing their conversation.

"What time are you getting back?" She breathed heavily. "I need you to confirm the new hires." She inhaled and exhaled slowly to control her heart rate.

"I told you not to hire anyone new. We'll have new girls in the spring. We can make do until then."

"No, we don't. We lost several girls to graduation, and we don't have enough girls to keep things running smoothly. The few we have can't handle our clien-"

LaShaun abruptly cut her off. "I don't want to talk about that right now. I need to meditate and get my head clear. We'll discuss it later."

Charlotte became perturbed and wrapped her ponytail around her hand. "Ok, do you," she stressed. "I'll be here keeping the train on the track, as usual."

"Watch that tone!" LaShaun hissed. "I said spring, and I meant it. Find a way to make it work." She made a kissing gesture and ended the call before Charlotte could reply.

Charlotte and LaShaun met during freshman orientation at Atlanta Presbyterian University and were fast friends. LaShaun entered the school on a one-year academic scholarship and was out of her element from the moment she stepped foot on the predominately white campus.

Thankfully, Charlotte was there to show her the ropes. Especially when LaShaun's scholarship ran out, leaving her clueless about where the money would come from for her to complete her degree and find a place to stay.

Charlotte, who also had to pay her own way through college,

was happy to provide a possible solution when all LaShaun's other efforts failed.

"The only way for you to stay in school is to be a Sugar Baby," Charlotte had told her.

"A Sugar Baby? What's that?"

"A Sugar Baby is someone who knows how to use their money-makers to get what they want, girl." Charlotte's cunning glare toggled up and down LaShaun's body. "You need the money; use what your momma gave ya."

Charlotte had been speaking, but it was Sadie's voice LaShaun heard. Also, Lucille had died months earlier, and she had no family that she knew of and no one she was accountable to, so she hadn't needed much convincing. She promptly heeded her advice but initially agreed to dates only, no sex. When that changed, she began making serious bank.

In her junior year, she transferred to Atlanta University and pledged to Alpha Rho Theta Sorority. A couple of her sorority sisters found out what she was doing and begged her to allow them to become Sugar Babies, too. She turned them down on multiple occasions before she finally obliged.

In return for connecting them with wealthy "benefactors," she kept a portion of each girl's payment as a finder's fee. Their business was steady and profitable. Consequently, when she graduated with her business degree, she had no debt and a nest egg sizeable enough to start a tax-paying business to wash her money...and *Sweet Dreams Boutique* was born.

The upscale lingerie boutique by day is a sex-for-hire escort ring by night. Launched in 2006 as a members-only boutique, it is now in several major cities, serving elite clientele from all over the world.

LaShaun pulled into the church's parking lot and drove to her designated parking space. "Lady LaShaun Delaney" was printed on paper that covered the metal sign containing the actual first lady's name.

Knowing all eyes would be on her, she put the car in park and took one last look in the mirror. Then, after checking her lipstick for smudges and running her fingers through her long curly honey-blond hair, the falcon wings on her vehicle flew up, and she exited the vehicle.

Although Christmas was two weeks away, the weather hadn't changed from Fall to Winter. As such, the ivory, double-breasted, Alexander McQueen dress she'd chosen to wear was perfect. It accentuated the body many compared to a modern supermodel; tall, slender, but curvy in all the right places.

As she strutted the ten feet to the door in her Jimmy Choo's, she was careful to keep her head high and back straight. She smiled and waved to the women clustered around their cars, sneaking glances in her direction.

Many churches were closed due to Covid-19, but DMI and others of similar size remained open. Each practiced proper social distancing and required congregants to wear masks and register for each service beforehand. Those who didn't attend in-person watched online.

When the greeter opened the door, LaShaun entered the massive U-shaped vestibule. Immediately, a hush fell over the women gathered around the sign-in table and refreshment station. They relaxed, and some even exhaled when Lashaun smiled brightly and greeted them collectively.

She scanned the area that held four six feet tables placed an adequate distance apart and centrally located between the refreshment station spanning the left wall and twelve shelves containing various pamphlets on the right wall. The three-thousand-seat sanctuary was thirty feet behind the tables.

Although the sanctuary doors were open, women stood around talking and enjoying each other's company. Thankfully, her attendant rushed her away before any of them approached her.

She needed time to meditate before delivering the message from Galatians 6:7, *"Don't expect to take out what you're not willing to put in."*

Chapter Two
ALL THAT GLITTERS

Karisma Stanley was attending the *Women of Worth* conference for the first time and was bursting with excitement! She would finally get to hear and meet LaShaun Delaney, the person she'd idolized for years.

She'd religiously followed her on social media and listened to her "*Called to Soar*" podcast. Although she wasn't a Christian herself, LaShaun's messages resonated with her. So, she didn't view them as sermons. To her, they were motivational speeches. And they'd gotten her through a very dark time in her life.

In sixth grade, Karisma overgeneralized and personalized every situation to the point where she didn't believe she was loved by anyone or capable of achieving anything. She was too boyish for her mother and too prissy for the students at school.

The girls would torment her with questions like, "Why do you talk like a white person?" or "You must think you're better than us?" Then, they would shove her as they walked down the hallway and dare her to do anything about it.

When it first happened, she told her mom, who alerted the principal. In retaliation, she was beaten in the school's bathroom by a gang of girls and spat on as they left her in a fetal position near the trash can. "And you better keep your mouth shut," the oldest and largest of the crew warned as they gave her a final sneer before leaving her in tears.

Sadly, Karisma's mom was worse than the students, belittling her for the smallest things. When she hadn't picked out Karisma's clothes, she'd bark, "Take off those jeans and put on a skirt." When Karisma combed her hair, she would say, "That style is ugly on you. You look a mess." Then, when the constant pressure to measure up caused Karisma's grades to drop, her mother beat her until welts formed on her body.

By eighth grade, Karisma was five feet three and one hundred twenty pounds. Her breasts and buttocks were fully formed, drawing stares and unwanted attention from her male peers. Fearing repercussions from other girls, she'd begged them to direct their attention elsewhere. But they refused. As a result, the girls intensified their taunts, and her life became unbearable.

In her first year of high school, she began cutting her wrists to relieve the pain. And, by junior year, cutting had become an addiction. She'd become so numb that she'd cut her arms, inner thighs, and other easily concealable body parts. To her, it seemed the weight lifted from her shoulders when blood flowed from her vein.

When her parents-Quinton and Deyja- learned she was depressed, they dismissed her cries for help as teenage theatrics. "You don't have bills to pay, you've got a roof over your head, and we give you everything you ask for...you don't have a reason to be unhappy," her mother admonished.

As if that wasn't enough, Karisma's father advised, "Just go out and have some fun with your friends. It will be alright." Unfortunately, they didn't appreciate the magnitude of her illness until they found her passed out on the bed from cutting herself too deeply.

Near the end of her junior year, final exams were underway. Having scored less than she desired on the SAT, she knew she needed to ace her tests to get into the college of her choice. But, having studied late into the night, she was exhausted when the time for her exam arrived. Her teacher scolded her when she laid her head on her desk, and the day went downhill fast.

When she got home, she ran to her room, threw her books on the floor, and grabbed a razor from beneath her mattress. She cut herself aggressively as the day's events rushed through her mind.

She knew she needed to tie something around her wrist and grab the first-aid kit to contain the blood flow, but she couldn't do it. She was tired of the mental anguish she experienced at school and home. She wanted to end it all.

A few minutes later, Deyja arrived and called to her from downstairs. Karisma opened her mouth to answer but couldn't utter a sound.

"Karisma, I know you hear me!" Don't make me come up there." Karisma's head fell limply, and her eyes began to close. Before long, she drifted out of consciousness.

Deyja stomped up the fifteen stairs to Karisma's room, expecting to find her at her desk with headphones on her ears. "Karisma!" she yelled as she reached the door and turned the knob. The door was locked, which angered her more.

She bammed on the door with balled-up fists. "Karisma, open this door!"

Karisma still didn't answer. Deyja pushed and pulled the doorknob multiple times. But the door wouldn't open. Then, her senses began to tingle, and fear washed over her. She remembered how depressed Karisma had been and called out frantically, "Karisma, you hear me, baby? Answer me!"

Not hearing a sound, she used her smartwatch to quickly call her husband. Then, she whacked the door faster and harder. When Quinton didn't answer, she left an urgent message on his voicemail. As her pulse raced and anxiety increased, she rushed to her bedroom to retrieve the door key from her jewelry box.

Bawling, she opened it and ran her hands through the jewelry on the top tray, but it wasn't there.

"Where is it?" she cried hysterically and poured its contents onto the floor. Then, using her hands to separate the pieces quickly, she saw the key amid her gold watches and antique rings.

She quickly used her left hand to wipe the mucous running from her nose as she snatched the key from the floor with her right. With a feeling of dread, she sprinted out of the room, bumping her shoulder on the door as she went.

When she finally reached the room and unlocked the door, she found Karisma slumped over onto her pillow; unresponsive.

Days later, Karisma woke up in the hospital surrounded by mental health professionals, blessed to be alive. Although she tried, she had trouble remembering all that had taken place. The treating physician said that her mother's quick thinking, and the life-sustaining measures she employed, saved her life.

Subsequently, after years of suffering in silence, Karisma started receiving the help she desperately needed. And it was a long hard road to recovery.

When LaShaun took the pulpit, Karisma and the women in attendance stood and applauded.

She looked heavenly standing behind the big clear podium, poised and waving at her admirers.

The light reflecting from the stained-glass windows onto her golden highlights gave her an angelic glow. When she walked from one side of the stage to the other, it seemed she floated on air.

When she shouted, "Praise the Lord Saints," the crowd erupted with, "Praise the Lord," as they clapped louder. After a round of chants, LaShaun held both her arms outstretched and motioned her hands up and down, signaling everyone to take their seats. When the women began to acquiesce, she soothingly and softly said over and over, All glory to God. All glory to God." After the applause died down, LaShaun began to speak.

Karisma carefully studied every gesture and listened to every word as Lashaun delivered her message. She had received three years of intensive therapy and now had the tools to envision herself on stage, admired by all.

She saw thousands of women rising and saying to her "You on it!" and "Say that!" as she awed them with her knowledge and wit.

Dr. Walker-her therapist taught her the power of visualization. He'd also taught her how to refute every lie her mind fed her and reframe it with a life-affirming truth. And with his guidance, she graduated high school on time and enrolled in a two-year college. She completed her Associate degree with honors and now was in her first semester at Atlanta University.

LaShaun was nearing the close of her message when Karisma snapped out of the reverie. Upset that she'd zoned out and missed the last of LaShaun's talking points, she scanned the program, noting that recordings of her teachings were available for purchase during the meet-and-greet. Then, anxious to be near the front of the receiving line, she hopped from her seat and bolted from the room to the next location before the room emptied.

As she opened the door and walked onto the back lawn where the meet and greet would take place, she saw at least a hundred women were already in line. They flooded the enormous white tent, and more were entering the line from the other side of the lawn.

She thought about turning around and leaving, but she'd spent fifty dollars to attend and three hundred dollars for the pink sundress and nude designer stilettos she wore. So, instead, she decided to pass the time by listening to an audiobook.

When her feet began to ache, she chastised herself for wearing such impractical shoes to a women's conference. She had never been to one before, but it didn't take a rocket scientist to know there would be a lot of standing.

She considered removing them but instantly heard her mom's voice admonish, "You better not put your bare feet on that ground. You're gonna get worms." Deyja was miles away, but her voice was as clear as it would be if she were standing beside her.

When she neared the front of the line, she felt a tap on her back. Taking her earbuds out, she turned to face a young woman she'd seen before but couldn't recall when or where. "I'm sorry to bother you," she said. "May I have a piece of gum? My throat's dry."

"Sure, hold on." Karisma dug in her conference tote bag, pulled out a pack of gum, and handed it to her.

"You're Karisma, right?" She pulled a piece from the packet. Karisma furrowed her brow as she tried to remember her name and where she'd met her.

"Yes," she answered.

Seeing the confused look on Karisma's face, the young lady said, "I'm Heiress Storm. *We met during Rush the other night, remember?*"

Karisma's eyes bulged as she remembered their first encounter. Now, she was horrified she'd forgotten such an important person so soon after meeting her. But short-term memory loss was an unfortunate side effect of her anxiety medication.

"Yes, I remember," she said hurriedly. "You're a Work of Art."

Heiress is the outgoing president of Alpha Rho Theta Sorority, and a *"Work of Art"* is the name used to refer to its members. Karisma attended Rush Week, along with many hopeful girls who expressed their interest. But, careful not to violate any unknown rules by striking up a conversation with Heiress, she inquired coyishly, "Is it okay for me to talk to you"?

Heiress chuckled and said, "Sure, it's okay! Just don't ask me anything about Alpha Rho."

Karisma relaxed and responded. "I would never. Did you enjoy the message?"

"I did. I was Lady Delaney's assistant at DMI, and I've heard her speak many times."

Karisma placed her hands to her mouth in awe. "You are so lucky!"

"I'm better than lucky. I'm blessed!" Heiress said emphatically.

"When I graduated from AU, she gave me the seed money to open a designer purse boutique here in Augusta. Its grand opening is in two days. You should come." Now beaming with pride, she cupped her right hand and pointed it towards the sky as she said, "It's called *Queen Heir Purse Boutique.*" Her hand punched the air as she said each word.

"Wow! That's a nice name. And that's very generous of her."

"I know," Heiress gloated. "She's like that with all the Sorors. She'll do anything to help us succeed."

They engaged in easy conversation as the line moved slowly. Karisma noted her pleasant and personable demeanor as they conversed about various topics and was glad she'd chosen to become a Work of Art herself one day.

When it was her turn to meet LaShaun, Karisma was petrified, and her feet were inexplicably glued to the floor. Thankfully, Heiress gave her a gentle nudge to move her forward. So, she took a deep breath, plastered a huge smile on her face, and approached LaShaun with her right hand outstretched.

"Hello, I'm Karisma Stanley. I enjoyed your message," she stated nervously.

"Well, thank you," LaShaun answered gracefully. I pray you were blessed by it."

"I sure was!" Karisma was immediately at ease. LaShaun was more approachable than she'd thought she would be. Her warm spirit gave Karisma the courage to add, "I'm a junior at AU, and I plan to visit DMI after Christmas break."

Still holding Karisma's hands in hers, LaShaun smiled. "Well, I look forward to seeing you there. Good luck this semester."

As Karisma thanked her, Heiress approached them and playfully bumped her hip against Karisma's hip. "A lot of people are waiting," she said chuckling as she moved her aside. Karisma grinned and replied, "I'm going...I'm going."

"Good! But before you go, Lady Delaney is still looking for someone to replace me, and I think you'd be a great fit." She looked at LaShaun, wiggled her eyebrows, and smiled.

"That's so nice of you to think of me." She beamed as she turned to LaShaun. "I would love to work for you!"

LaShaun laughed at the exchange. "I can't promise you anything but come and see me when you return to school and we'll discuss it."

Karisma clapped her hands giddily. "I sure will! Thank you!" Then, she turned to Heiress and gave her a fist bump. "Thank you, too, Heiress! I really appreciate it."

"You're welcome. Now go on over there and buy some merch." With her hands, Heiress pretended to sweep her away.

Karisma told them goodbye and went to the product table. After purchasing a recording of the message and a *Called to Soar sweatshirt*, she leaned on the nearest wall to watch as LaShaun greeted the other conference attendees. When the last person shook her hand, a hostess announced the end of the meet-and-greet.

On the long walk to her car, Karisma had time to reflect on what had transpired during the last few hours. She didn't know why, but as she hopped in her car, she said, "Thank You for letting me meet LaShaun Delaney. Help me to be just like her."

Immediately, she heard Deyja's voice warn, "All that glitters, ain't gold."

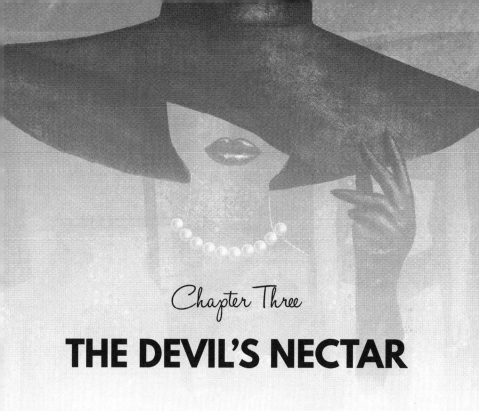

Chapter Three
THE DEVIL'S NECTAR

Immediately following the end of the meet-and-greet, LaShaun returned to her car, kicked off her heels, and released the energy rushing through her body. The conference already a distant memory, she began to focus on *Sweet Dreams Boutique*.

She wanted to wait until the new Works of Art were initiated before bringing in more girls to the Boutique, but that may not be possible. Sex is the only business that thrives during depression, oppression, and regression, so she may have to pull some of her undergrad Sorors sooner rather than later.

When she and Langston married, she thought about relinquishing *Sweet Dreams Boutique* to Charlotte completely, but she was too afraid to do so. She'd worked hard to obtain financial freedom, and she'd seen how men mistreated women who depended on them for survival.

So, not wanting to jeopardize her financial security for someone whose feelings could change at any time, LaShaun decided to become a silent partner instead. She continued to manage the finances while allowing Charlotte to handle the day-to-day operations.

When she rounded the corner to her home, she was pleased to see Langston standing on the porch, awaiting her arrival. He was a sight for sore eyes, as the older women in the congregation reminded her each Sunday.

His black designer jogging suit perfectly accentuated his tall, muscular body. When her eyes took in his dark velvety skin, short, cropped goatee, and megawatt smile, butterflies danced in her stomach. She was married to the man that caused every woman in the church-both young and old- to think about the many ways they could sin.

After LaShaun eased the car into the garage, he strolled over to her with a boyish grin. The one that meant he was ready for an evening of romance. As she parked the car, he opened the door and bent down to kiss her before she could exit the vehicle.

"Hey, you!" LaShaun purred as Langston took her hand and helped her out of her seat. Then, barely leaving enough room for air to come between them, he whispered, "Welcome home," as he embraced her in his arms.

"It's good to be home. Being in your arms is even better." So, she stayed there, enjoying the warmth of his tongue now racing across the tip of her earlobe.

"You're gonna get us in trouble if you don't let me go."

"Oh, I love trouble," LaShaun crooned. Then she stood on her toes and took Langston's bottom lip between hers, slowly drawing it into her mouth. She sucked gently before capturing his tongue and allowing it to tango with hers. After a long passionate kiss, he pulled his arms away and stepped back.

"You need to get in the house before we get arrested," he said lustfully.

"I'll be waiting inside," she purred while sliding her fingers across his chest and maneuvering around him to enter the house.

Shaking his head, he smiled widely and straightened his jogging pants before unloading her things from the car.

LaShaun strolled into the house and headed to the closet inside her bathroom, where she grabbed her silk robe. It was no surprise that Langston had a nice, hot bubble bath waiting for her. The immersion water heater kept the water at just the right temperature.

He'd placed candles strategically throughout the bathroom. Chocolate-covered strawberries and alcohol-free wine sat on a serving platter near the tub, and their date-night playlist streamed from the Bluetooth speaker. LaShaun hummed along to Kem's *Love Calls* as she applied makeup remover to her face.

After she disrobed, he entered the bathroom and embraced her from behind. They swayed to the music as he used his right hand to caress her body while singing softly in her ear.

"You're trying to heat things up, I see," LaShaun moaned.

"I'm only trying to finish what you started."

LaShaun coyishly moved away from his reach. "Sir, I have to get into this hot bath my man ran for me before it gets cold, and you are hindering my progress."

"Oh, it's like that?" Langston thrust his hand over his heart as if it was wounded. Then, biting his lower lip and staring at her in the way he knew she couldn't resist, he said, "I'll tell you what, baby. Take your time and enjoy your soak. I have something even better waiting when you get out."

As she fanned herself with her right hand, he slowly swaggered out of the restroom, leaving a smoldering fire in all the right places. It was going to be a passionate end to a beautiful day.

LaShaun was gently awakened by Rosa, her live-in house manager of ten years. She'd been taking care of Langston and LaShaun for so long that they treated her like family.

With her eyes closed, LaShaun slid her hand to the other side of the bed, expecting to feel Langston's warm, comforting body. But his spot was empty.

"Mr. Delaney had a meeting," Rosa informed as she watched her pat the bed with her hands. "He didn't want to wake you."

LaShaun's eyes shot open, and she turned her head toward Rosa. "What kind of meeting?"

Curtly, Rosa replied, "That's not my place to ask." She opened the drapery.

"My, aren't you helpful," LaShaun retorted sarcastically. On most days, they bantered back and forth, but today Rosa ignored LaShaun's usual morning grumpiness.

"Your breakfast will be waiting when you come downstairs," Rosa told her as she hurried out of the room and closed the door.

Reluctantly, LaShaun got out the bed and headed for the shower. Inside, she allowed the water to heat as she hit play on her worship playlist and applied her purifying face mask. Then, stepping into her steaming refuge, she let the perfectly heated water massage her scalp, shoulders, and back. Her senses came to life as she completed her morning ritual.

After showering, she conditioned her hair and quickly dressed.

The smell of bacon and coffee filled the room and had her salivating. When she entered the kitchen, she grabbed a slice of bacon, a warm blueberry muffin, and salted caramel coffee from the kitchen counter. She then hugged Rosa, thanked her, and dashed out the door.

She got in her car and tried to reach Langston, but the call went straight to voice mail. Then she called Charlotte, but she didn't answer either. Her spa appointment wasn't until ten o'clock, so she turned on her DMI App and listened to Langston's latest sermon as she drove to the boutique.

When she arrived, she entered through the private entrance so customers wouldn't see her. She tossed her purse on the mahogany desk, plopped in her chair, and increased the volume on the security monitor.

An elderly gentleman dressed in overalls, dark sunglasses, and a *Kangol* hat approached the counter. LaShaun snickered at the ridiculous disguise.

"How are you today?" He laid a black lace bustier, and a no-show thong made of sheer mesh on the counter.

"I'm doing fine, Sir Lancelot. And how are you?" Although the escort business had a members-only model, they never used a customer's real name.

"Doing well! Doc gave me a clean bill of health, and I feel like a man half my age."

He'd experienced a heart attack not long ago, and Charlotte looked at him with concern. "Are you sure you can handle Claudia tonight? We don't want another scare."

He chuckled lightheartedly. "Oh, I'm sure. When you taste the devil's nectar, you cannot help but go back for more." His loud, boisterous laugh filled the room.

Shaking her head, Charlotte called out his total, $3500. When he handed over his *American Express Centurion,* Charlotte quickly ran the transaction and grinned as he left the building. A few minutes later, when she walked to the office, she was startled to find LaShaun there.

"I didn't know you were coming in today." Charlotte approached LaShaun and pulled her into a tight embrace.

"I know. I was heading to the spa and decided to stop by to apologize for being abrupt when we last spoke."

Charlotte leaned over and picked up a folder from her desk. "No need. I learned how to ignore you long ago."

LaShaun's guilty conscience welcomed Charlotte's sincere tone. "Thanks for understanding. I have a spa appointment so I can't stay. We'll talk later."

Charlotte shook her head in disagreement. "Not so fast...we need to discuss recruitment."

LaShaun's cell rang before she could protest. She took it from her purse and looked at the screen. The smile that crept across her face was so deep, she was positive it was all in her voice. "Hey, my love. Where were you off to so early this morning?"

Charlotte's jaw clenched as Langston's deep voice barreled over the line. "I met some ministers on the golf course."

"Oh, okay. Where are you now?"

"Heading home. You're going to the spa, right? Do you want to meet me for lunch?"

LaShaun moved the phone from her mouth as she whispered to Charlotte and pointed at the phone. "Langston. I gotta run." She turned hurriedly and walked out before seeing the scowl on Charlotte's face.

"Yes, we can meet at one o'clock. Our usual spot?"

"Sounds good, babe. Enjoy your massage."

"I will. Love you."

"Love you, too." Langston terminated the call.

LaShaun felt a familiar tug in her spirit that she'd been wrestling with for years. The guilt of constantly hiding beneath a bed of lies to cover the behind-the-scenes dealings of the Boutique. Although she'd wanted to many times, she'd never found the strength to tell him the truth.

They'd met one night after a belligerent client had become so intoxicated that he physically abused a *Dream Girl*. Langston was among the few black men in attendance at the corporate party and came to her rescue as others pretended not to notice. However, when the man continued to charge at the Dream Girl despite Langston's attempt to stop him, Langston knocked him unconscious.

Although the party's host wanted Langston and the young girl to leave quietly, Langston tried to convince her to call the police and file charges. But she refused, asking him to call LaShaun instead. Langston did as she requested and stayed with her until LaShaun arrived.

From the moment he laid eyes on LaShaun, he was mesmerized by her beauty and how she handled the young lady with such concern and compassion. Instantly, he fell in love with her, knowing she would be his wife.

Three months after they met, he showed up at the boutique with a bouquet of roses in hand and proposed to a stunned LaShaun. Soon after getting engaged, they were married at the courthouse. One year later, Langston answered his call to ministry.

By the time they said, "*I do*," LaShaun was in too deep to turn her back on the Dream Girls, Charlotte, or the business. Now, twelve years later, Langston is still clueless.

After her massage and facial, LaShaun met Langston at their favorite seafood restaurant. Then, they spent the rest of their day binge-watching television shows while relaxing in bed. By nine o'clock, they both were asleep. They were both dreaming when Langston's phone startled them awake.

"In the hospital?" What happened? Have you seen him?" Langston paused, listening for a moment before he said, "I'm on the way!" Then, he sprang from the bed and rushed to his closet, with LaShaun on his heels.

"What's wrong?" Charlotte asked, alarmed.

"It's Deacon Thomas," Langston stammered. "He was rushed to the emergency room in critical condition."

"Wait on me. I'm coming with you." LaShaun scrambled to find something to wear. She had no idea she was about to visit the man who could ruin her marriage and Sweet Dreams Boutique.

Chapter Four
A SERIOUS MATTER

LaShaun looked around the waiting room at all the families whose loved ones were in surgery, and her heart ached for them. It was the Christmas season, but the lifeless gray walls, frigid temperature, and nauseating smell of antiseptics were reminiscent of Halloween.

Deacon Thomas' daughter, Kari, rested her head on LaShaun's shoulder as Kairo, his son, stood against the wall and talked on the phone to an out-of-town family member. Langston walked up and down the hallway as he updated members of the Deacon's Board.

LaShaun did her best to be the comfort they all needed during this dreadful experience. She couldn't believe Deacon Thomas had been in surgery for six hours. He was still fighting for his life.

Unlike most in the congregation, he was always armed with a kind and encouraging word when they spoke. When she and Langston hit a rough patch early in their marriage, it was Deacon

Thomas and his wife who rallied behind them. LaShaun smiled as she recalled how the seasoned couple fought for them when they didn't have the strength or will to fight for themselves.

Just a year ago, they'd lost Sister Thomas to cancer. Deacon Thomas tried to carry on bravely, but LaShaun still saw unbridled grief and loneliness when she looked in his eyes. Now, there was a possibility they'd lose him, too. If that happened, the ministry would never be the same.

"Thank you for coming," Kari told LaShaun for the fourth time. It was as if her mind was stuck on repeat, incapable of forming any other sentence. She was scheduled to graduate college in the Spring but postponed her final classes to take care of her father after his initial heart attack. Always a daddy's girl, she rarely left his side.

LaShaun gently squeezed her hands and glanced at her watch. It was nine forty-five. The cafeteria would stop serving breakfast at ten.

"You need to put something on your stomach." LaShaun patted her hand. "What would you like from the cafeteria?"

"I can't eat anything...my stomach is in knots," Kari muttered. She was so inconsolable when LaShaun and Langston arrived, that LaShaun gave her something to calm her nerves. She'd stopped pacing the floor and demanding answers from the nurses, but her emotions were still high.

LaShaun grabbed some tissue from her purse and handed it to her, replacing the tattered tissue she'd been clenching for hours.

"Try to remain positive," LaShaun said. "Everything's going to be all right. God is in that room guiding the surgeons as we speak."

Kairo walked over and sat beside Kari, nodding in agreement. He was visibly shaken, but LaShaun could tell he was trying to be strong for his twin. She remembered Sister Thomas saying how

Kairo was born two minutes before Kari, and how seriously he assumed the role of *big brother*.

Langston peeked into the room from the hallway and caught LaShaun's eye. She excused herself and got up to meet him. Distraught, he held onto her like they hadn't seen each other in years.

"I can't believe this is happening," LaShaun said.

"I know, it's shocking for all of us." Langston continued holding her tightly. She wondered if he was doing it for her benefit or his own. Deacon Thomas was Langston's right hand at the church. He was no-nonsense and knew the Bible well enough to shut down the foolishness of any deacon on staff who didn't...which was most of them.

Langston finally released LaShaun, guiding her further away from the twins, making sure they weren't within earshot.

"Have you been able to get any information from the doctor?"

Langston's grim face answered before he did. "We don't have all the particulars yet, but as you know, he was already unconscious for a while by the time the paramedics reached him. There's brain rhythm, but it doesn't look good."

"Even now, He's the God who heals," LaShaun declared.

"Yes, He is." Langston pecked LaShaun on the forehead. Simultaneously, their phones rang. LaShaun raised her index finger to indicate she was stepping away for privacy and walked in the opposite direction.

"Hey Charlotte," she answered.

"Hey, can you talk?"

"Only for a minute; what's going on?"

"I got a call from Detective Cruz this morning. When he arrived at the station, he found out someone had been rushed to the hospital early this morning from the Lancaster hotel. He doesn't have a name, but he believes it was one of our clients."

LaShaun's stomach dropped. Detective Cruz was one of their closest allies on the police force. He kept them informed of anything that could jeopardize their business, and he knew the Lancaster Hotel was where the *Dream Girls* met their clients.

"Please don't tell me that," LaShaun responded dreadfully. "I'm at the hospital right now, checking on one of our deacons. He was found unconscious around that time!"

"Was he found at a hotel?"

"I don't know. But when they found him, he was unconscious. That's too much of a coincidence."

"Don't jump to conclusions." Charlotte's calming voice did nothing to make LaShaun's heart stop racing. "Detective Cruz is going to call me back once he's able to get some additional information. Now, is that deacon of yours wealthy enough to gain membership?"

"Absolutely! He is Atlanta's past mayor, owns three car dealerships, and inherited several car washes from his father. Which one of our girls was at the hotel last night?"

"Claudia. I've called several times, but I can't reach her."

"Well, keep trying, and hit me back when you know more."

"Will do."

"Bye." *Lord, please don't let it be Deacon Thomas.* As she turned back to Langston, his strained expression stopped her in her tracks. "What's wrong?"

"I just spoke with a member of our security team, and he gave me sensitive information regarding Deacon Thomas."

LaShaun's heart pounded against her chest. "What is it?"

"Don't repeat this to anyone," he cautioned.

"Of course."

SWEET DREAMS BOUTIQUE

Langston moved closer and lowered his voice. "Deacon Thomas was found at the Lancaster Hotel butt naked, with a dog collar tied around his neck."

LaShaun tried responding, but her brain shut down, her mouth went dry, and everything faded to black. Luckily, Langston caught her before she hit the floor.

A while later, she awakened to find herself hooked to an IV. Langston was praying as he held her hands.

"Where am I?" Her head was still foggy.

Langston lifted his head. "Oh, thank God you're awake! Let me get the doctor." He rushed out of the room and quickly returned with a tall, handsome, middle-aged physician.

"Baby, this is Dr. Champion. He'll explain what happened to you."

"Hi, Mrs. Delaney," he said somberly. "You gave us quite the scare." The seriousness of his tone caused her heart rate to increase.

"What's going on with me, Doctor?" Langston walked over and grabbed her hand. He caressed it with his thumb as the doctor answered her.

"You fainted a short while ago. Normally, fainting isn't a cause for hospitalization; however, you were exhibiting signs of tachycardia."

"What does that mean?" LaShaun was alarmed.

"Simply put, you fainted because your heart rate was dangerously elevated. Thankfully, you were here at the hospital when it happened, and we were able to act quickly, implementing emergency protocols. That said, we expect a complete recovery."

"When can I go home?"

"We're going to need to monitor you overnight and continue giving you fluids to keep you hydrated. You should be able to go home tomorrow."

"So, there's no long-term damage?"

"No ma'am, you're in good health. Everything will be fine, but you still need to follow up with your primary care physician."

"Thank you," LaShaun gasped, relieved.

"Get some rest, and I will return tomorrow during rounds."

"I will." A single tear fell from the corner of LaShaun's eye, taking its time to reach the pillow.

Langston walked out of the room with the doctor, giving LaShaun a moment to gather her thoughts. Although she was relieved to be fine, the stress of what caused her to faint in the first place made her sad all over again. She was lost in her thoughts when Langston returned.

"Don't scare me like that again." He bent and kissed her.

"It wasn't my idea," she said somberly.

He gently wiped her tears with a monogrammed handkerchief he pulled from his pocket. "Are you hurting? Can I get you anything?"

"No, baby. I'm just glad you're here. I was just thinking about Deacon Thomas. Is there any news?"

Langston sighed. "He made it through surgery, but he's not out of the woods yet. We're trying to remain positive."

"I hate this happened to him. He means the world to me."

Langston flashed a sympathetic smile. "I know he does. And if you could heal him, it would already be done. But he's in God's hands now. All we can do is pray."

There was a knock at the door, then it slowly creaked open. LaShaun looked up to see Charlotte hesitantly walking in. Langston rose to greet her.

"Is it alright to come in?"

"Sure, this one here's been waiting to see you."

You have no idea, LaShaun thought as Charlotte rushed over to her bedside. She bent to hug LaShaun. "I'm so glad you're okay. I don't know what I'd do without you," she said.

"There's no need to worry. The doctor said I'll be fine."

Langston walked over and slid a chair over so Charlotte could sit beside LaShaun's bed. He then walked to the foot of the bed, where he stood as he reiterated to Charlotte what the doctor said. After they briefly discussed her condition, he went to the head of the bed and kissed LaShaun on her lips.

"Babe, several members rushed here when they heard the news about you and Deacon Thomas, and they're in the waiting room. I'm going to let them know how you're doing."

LaShaun was surprised at the news. "Oh, ok. Please thank them for me. How are Kairo and Kari?"

"They're hanging in there. Family members arrived a short while ago and convinced them to go home and shower. I'll be sure to let them know you're alright when they return."

"Thanks. Be sure to tell them I love them."

"I will. Goodbye, Charlotte." He touched her on the shoulder before exiting the room. Charlotte flinched.

LaShaun was grateful for the privacy. She peered at Charlotte with grave concern. "What did you find out? Please tell me Deacon Thomas wasn't with Claudia when this happened to him."

"I wish I could," Charlotte's head shook furiously. "He was the last customer I rang up when you were in the office the other day. Do you remember the older gentleman with the Kangol hat?"

LaShaun closed her eyes and sighed heavily. "I had no idea that was him. I can't believe I didn't recognize his voice."

"Yep. It seems the good deacon liked the taste of the devil's nectar a little too much." Charlotte flashed a mischievous grin.

LaShaun lightly popped Charlotte's hand. "This is a serious

matter," she giggled despite herself. "How was he even able to make it through screening? Our vetting process is airtight."

"It is, but church affiliation isn't investigated," Charlotte explained defensively. "It would be if you were more involved in the day-to-day operations, but you're not. And protecting the church isn't my concern."

"Well, it should be. He shouldn't have passed the background check!" LaShaun's heart rate sped up, causing the monitor to beep frantically.

"Calm down," Charlotte coaxed. "It's clear something slipped through the cracks. Our head of security is looking into it, and I should know something later today."

Charlotte opened her mouth to say more but stopped as a nurse entered the room. After checking her vitals and ensuring LaShaun wasn't in any danger, she left.

"We don't have time to wait until later," LaShaun spat, "we've got to contain this immediately."

Charlotte's eyes grew wide. "Who are you telling? Detective Cruz came by the boutique to advise an investigation is underway. They're trying to find out who tied him to the bedposts. Right now, they have no clue Claudia was there. We have to keep it that way."

LaShaun laid her hand on her chest and exhaled. Charlotte continued.

"They have no leads, and their investigation is at a standstill. But they're waiting to talk to *Sir Lancelot*." Charlotte emphasized Deacon Thomas's alias with air quotes, trying to lighten LaShaun's spirit, but it had the opposite effect.

"Don't call him that. Put some respect on his name," LaShaun said forcefully.

"I'm sorry." Charlotte straightened up and put on a solemn face.

"Listen, this isn't the time to think of this man as someone you love. In this situation, he's not the deacon you know, he's someone who can bring our entire operation down."

"You know I can't do that!" LaShaun protested vehemently.

"I know you're praying for him to pull through, and I am too. Believe me - I don't want anything worse to happen to him." Charlotte's eyes turned dark. "I care, I really do. But if it comes down to that man's double life or us, I will choose us every time. You need that same mentality. You have in the past."

"I know," LaShaun conceded. "Prayerfully when he is conscious, either he won't remember what happened, or he'll be too humiliated to tell anyone what he was engaged in."

The door opened again, and Langston came back into the room. When Charlotte reached down to give LaShaun a goodbye hug, she warned, "You better pray hard."

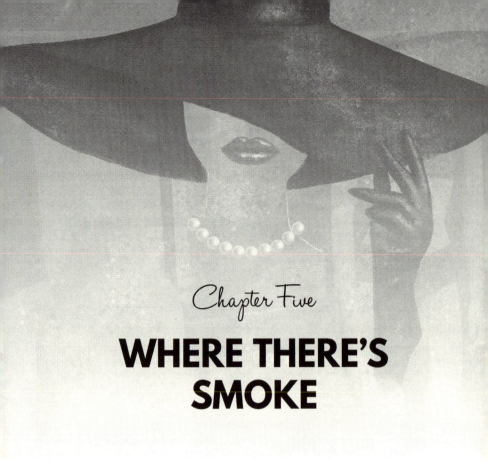

Chapter Five

WHERE THERE'S SMOKE

Heiress stood in the middle of Queen Heir Purse Boutique and admired the myriad of designer purses on display. Yesterday's grand opening had been a smashing success, with the mayor, councilmen, and three hundred of Augusta's finest citizens attending the ribbon cutting. Half of her inventory had been purchased during the six-hour mega sale, and she'd made a replacement order last night.

As she waited for the first customers of the day, she sprayed the glass display cases and cleaned them of fingerprints and smudges. When she finished, her cell phone rang.

"Good morning, thanks for calling Queen Heir Purse Boutique. This is Heiress. How may I assist you?"

"Heiress, this is Claudia; I need to speak with Soror Delaney." Heiress heard trepidation dripping through Claudia's panicked voice.

"I'm not in Atlanta, you'll have to call her cell. Is everything okay?"

"Thanks." Claudia abruptly ended the call.

Perplexed, Heiress sat on her lilac velvet sofa and dialed LaShaun. Her secretary - Ms. Smith, intercepted the call. Heiress cleared her throat and steadied her voice. "Hi Ms. Smith, this is Heiress. I can't reach Lady Delaney, is she there?"

"Hi, Heiress. She's in a meeting. Can I take a message?"

"Umm...I received a call from someone who works at the boutique, and I need to talk directly to her. Have her call me when she's free, please. It's urgent."

"The meeting is scheduled for another hour. If it's urgent, you should contact Charlotte," Ms. Smith responded sternly.

Heiress hesitated. She didn't get a good vibe from Charlotte and always avoided engaging in a conversation with her. However, if Claudia was in trouble, she didn't have a choice.

"Yes, Ma'am. I'll call her. Still have Lady Delaney call me when she's free." When the call ended, she immediately dialed Charlotte, who surprisingly answered on the first ring.

"Hey Charlotte, this is Heiress. Claudia just called asking for Lady Delaney, but she's in a meeting. It seemed like she was freaking out over something. Mrs. Smith suggested I call you since LaShaun's unavailable."

Charlotte exhaled. Claudia contacted her last night in a panic and was instructed to go to a hotel to lay low. This morning, Charlotte arranged for her to take a flight to Miami until the situation regarding the deacon was handled. Although Claudia agreed, she never boarded the plane.

Calmly, Charlotte questioned Heiress. "When did she call? Did she give her location?"

"No. The call lasted all of two seconds. Is everything okay?"

Charlotte, like Claudia, ignored the question. "Thanks, Heiress. I'll see if I can reach her." Charlotte immediately disconnected the call.

Ever the worrier, Heiress couldn't focus on anything other than Claudia when the call ended. She tried to reach her again, but her phone went straight to voicemail. As she prepared to contact Claudia's roommate, her friend Tara called via FaceTime.

"Hey Chick," Tara chirped. "You busy?"

Heiress looked at her watch and pulled out a blueberry muffin she picked up from a local bakery. "No, I'm eating breakfast. What's up?"

Moving her hands to emphasize her words, Tara blurted, "*Girl!* How 'bout I saw Claudia outside the club last night looking tore up from the floor up!"

Heiress put her muffin on the glass coffee table in front of the sofa. "Are you sure it was her?"

"Of course, I am!" Tara frowned. "Her hair was wild, she was hiding behind cars, and it looked like she was dodging someone." Her head shook with pity. "I tried to check on her, but she hopped into a white car before I could get close. The whole thing was crazy."

"Did you call out to her? Was she by herself?" Heiress was getting more alarmed by the minute.

"I called her name, but I guess she didn't hear me. She was alone but kept looking around like she was being followed." Tara put toothpaste on her toothbrush and began brushing her teeth.

"Why did you let her get away? You should have gone to her," Heiress scolded as she watched spittle and toothpaste fly.

"Do I look like the police to you?" she snapped after spitting in the sink and rinsing it down the drain. "Besides, she was dipping and dodging, honey. I couldn't have gotten to her if I wanted to...which I didn't." She rinsed with mouthwash and washed her face.

Heiress shook her head. "Something's going on. She called me this morning asking for Lady Delaney like she was too scared to let anyone hear her. I didn't even recognize it was her at first because the number was blocked."

"Dang, what has she gotten herself into?"

"I don't know. But when I called Charlotte, she had been looking for Claudia but was vague in her responses. She didn't tell me anything."

Pointing her finger at the screen, Tara replied, "See. I told you not to get hooked up with Charlotte and Lady Delaney. My uncle told me they're selling more than lingerie at that boutique. Claudia probably got caught up."

Heiress rolled her eyes. "I don't fool with Charlotte, and there is no way Lady Delaney is involved in something so shady," she defended.

Tara sucked her teeth. "See, you're too trusting. I put nothin' past nobody. A person is only as holy as their opportunities, and where there's smoke, there's fire."

Heiress snickered. "You're so extra. I'll call you later."

"Let me know if you find out anything," Tara hurriedly interjected.

"I will." She could not stay in Augusta selling purses while Claudia was potentially in danger.

Shortly before noon, she made it to her mother- Johnysa's, house to check on her before going to see LaShaun. She hadn't been to her childhood home since she moved to Augusta. She heard her mother yell out to her as soon as she unlocked the door and walked into the house.

"Heiress, is that you?"

"Yes ma'am." Heiress knew her mom had already seen her on the security camera. Heiress took off her shoes, left them on the mat by the door, and went down the long hall to her mother's bedroom. She passed the living room, kitchen, and a half bath before reaching her.

"Hand me those lottery tickets over there," Johnysa instructed from her bed as Heiress gave her a hug.

"Over where?"

"Where do you think? I only keep them in one place."

Heiress walked to the dresser by the door and picked up the tickets from the jewelry box. Her dresser was littered with everything from past due bills to porcelain bowls filled with dried, leftover food.

Johnysa hadn't gotten out of bed in three days. Dried mascara was smudged around the rims of her weary eyes, and her matted hair smelled of smoke. She looked every bit the torn woman who was mourning her impending divorce.

Hamilton-Heiress's father had hooked up with a younger woman, and a baby was on the way. Johnysa was so distraught, that she'd become clinically depressed. She temporarily closed her law practice and stayed in bed all day. Her best friend checked on her every day, but Heiress was exhausted trying to encourage her mother to move forward; her efforts were met with contempt.

"Here," she sniffed, handing the lottery tickets to Johnysa. Heiress watched in silence as the woman immediately went to vigorously scratch the opaque covering on each card. After winning nothing, Johnysa sighed and glared at Heiress.

"I need $257 for the light bill."

Heiress closed her eyes and pinched the bridge of her nose. "I just gave you $300 two days ago. What did you do with that?"

Johnysa was indignant. "Don't question me, girl! I'm your momma, you ain't mine."

If you're my momma, act like it. Stop laying on your butt and get back to work, Heiress wanted to scream. But she knew better, so she kept that sentiment to herself. "Why haven't you reopened your practice? You can't continue to lay in bed and do nothing. Dad's not coming back."

Johnysa stared at her and responded snarkily, "I don't want your daddy back. And, you know I'm not playing with Covid. *You* can run around like you're made of *Teflon,* but I'm protecting myself. I'll go back to work when it's safe...not a moment sooner. Now, are you giving me the money or not?"

The stress headache Heiress walked in with intensified. She squeezed her eyes shut and massaged her temples taking steady deep breaths.

"Mother...I...I don't have it," she sputtered.

"What you mean you don't have it?"

"I mean I don't have it. I'm moving into my condo in a few days, and I don't know how much I need for closing costs."

"Thanks for nothing." Johnysa turned her back and pulled the covers over her head.

Heiress went to her old bedroom, closed the blinds, and plopped down on her bed. All the excitement surrounding Claudia had triggered a migraine. She was concerned about Claudia and wanted to help her if she could, but the pain would worsen if she didn't take care of herself first. She took two CBD gummies, her migraine medicine, and prayed for Claudia as she waited for the medicine to take effect.

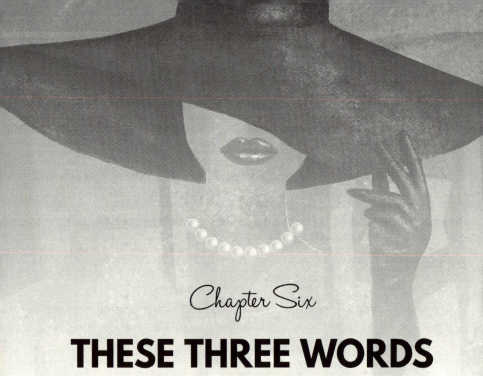

Chapter Six

THESE THREE WORDS

Christmas came and went without much fanfare, but Deacon Thomas died before the new year began. He was talking and making jokes with LaShaun that morning, but at ten o'clock that night she and Langston were informed he'd passed away. Due to the shocking turn of events, Kari convinced Kairo to request an autopsy. Now, the routine investigation to find the Deacon's escort has become a full-scale investigation to find his murderer. It was decided Charlotte would do everything in her power to ensure the investigation didn't lead to Claudia, and LaShaun would resume her duties at DMI. She focused on planning the Spring Women's Retreat and was thankful it kept her too busy to worry.

She was also grateful for Heiress's suggestion to hire Karisma. She started working in mid-January and had become a great asset. With the investigation into the deacon's death gaining momentum,

LaShaun's mind was all over the place. Karisma tackled small tasks while she focused on the major ones. Ms. Smith answered the phone, managed her schedule, and made sure no one bothered her.

Although Karisma loved working for LaShaun, she was disappointed with the solemn atmosphere in the office. LaShaun was nothing like the woman she'd created in her mind. She was expecting a lively soul who was approachable, and willing to pour wisdom into her. Instead, LaShaun was morose and antisocial.

Reporting to Ms. Smith didn't make things any better. The first thing the stern woman did was give her strict orders not to approach LaShaun unless she was instructed to do so. Then, she confined her to the conference room. When Karisma ventured to the restroom, Ms. Smith watched keenly.

Having worked at the church for a month, she'd yet to have a full conversation with LaShaun or anyone else at DMI. Most of her interactions consisted of taking papers to LaShaun's office and awaiting her signature and receiving stick-it notes from Ms. Smith.

She was immersed in filing papers when a detective entered the office. He spoke with Ms. Smith before making his way over to her. Ms. Smith's face looked as if she'd been chewing sour grapes, but Karisma was delighted to see him.

Hi, Ms. Stanley. I'm Detective Peterson from the Cobb County Police Department. Do you mind if I ask you a few questions?"

Karisma smiled brightly. "As long as it's okay with Ms. Smith, I'm fine with it. I thought you would meet me at my home, but this is just as good."

"I cleared it with Ms. Smith first." He took out a notepad and pen. "Were you expecting me?"

"Well, I knew the insurance company was sending out an investigator. I didn't know it would be a police detective."

The detective's confused face was jarring. "I'm not here regarding an insurance issue, Ms. Stanley."

"Then why are you here?"

"Ms. Stanley where were you on December 18th and 19th of 2019?" he asked, ignoring her question.

Karisma was perplexed. "It's hard to remember. Probably in my dorm room, I guess."

"Are you sure you weren't at the Lancaster Hotel?" The detective's tone turned abrasive. The unspoken accusation had her nervous.

"What? No!"

The man's brows narrowed. "Are you familiar with a man named Archibald Thomas?"

"N-no," Karisma stuttered. "I mean, I've heard his name on the news, but I don't know him."

"We have reason to believe your vehicle was seen fleeing the scene around one a.m. on December 19th. Do you know any reason why your car would be there, but you weren't."

Karisma was flabbergasted. Rod-her cousin borrowed her car that week, and she wasn't anywhere near it. He frequented a club down the street from the hotel, which explained why her car was in the vicinity, but because of his tumultuous relationship with the law, Karisma didn't mention it to the detective.

Rod always had one foot in jail and the other foot on a banana peel. Still, Karisma couldn't fathom how he would be connected to Deacon Thomas's case. *He would sell him some weed, but he wouldn't dare kill him. Would he?*

"Miss? Miss!" The detective nudged Karisma, snapping her from her thoughts.

"Sir?"

"I asked if you know this young lady?" He shoved a photo that had been screenshot from security camera footage in Karisma's face. Pretending to thoroughly examine it first, she shook her head.

"Are you sure you don't know this woman?" Again, he treated her as a suspect.

"I said I don't know her," Karisma reiterated, this time with more authority.

"Can you account for your whereabouts on December 27th?"

"It was the Christmas holidays, so I'm pretty sure I was at home with my family. Why are you asking me these questions?"

"Where is your home, Ms. Stanley?"

"Savannah, Georgia. And I'm not answering anymore of your questions without my parents or my attorney being present." She stared at the detective belligerently.

"You will regret that decision." The detective handed her his card and exited the building. A few minutes later, Karisma was summoned to LaShaun's office.

"Are you okay, Karisma? What did the detective want?" She gestured for her to sit in the lilac chair facing her. The bags beneath her eyes indicated a lack of sleep. Although she smiled, it did not mask the sadness in her eyes.

To keep from upsetting her any more than she already seemed, Karisma measured her words carefully. "I thought he was here to investigate my insurance claim, but he was investigating something else."

"What was that?"

"The death at the Lancaster Hotel."

LaShaun pretended to pick lint from her skirt. After a moment, she cleared her throat and placed her intertwined hands under her chin. "Well, I wish he would have spoken to me. I'm not sure if you are aware, but the person who died was a deacon at our church and very dear to me."

"Yes Ma'am, I'm sorry for your loss. I saw that online."

"Thank you. Why would he want to question you?"

"Because my car was seen near the crime scene the night he died."

LaShaun's eye twitched, but Karisma pretended not to notice. "Were you there Karisma?"

"No ma'am. I was at the dorm, studying for a makeup final."

"Then why would they think your car was there? If you know anything that can help the investigation, please tell me."

"He showed me a picture of a girl getting into a white car, but I didn't know her. My car was stolen around that time, so I don't know if it was mine or not."

"What kind of car do you have?"

"A white Honda Accord. It was at my mom's house, and someone stole it from the driveway. I filed a police report and an insurance claim. That's why I thought the detective was here about that."

LaShaun nodded. "I understand. Please let me know if you can think of anything to aid in the investigation. I won't rest until I know what happened to Deacon Thomas."

LaShaun turned her chair away from Karisma, took a Kleenex from the box on her sidebar, and wiped her eyes. Suddenly, Karisma's throat became dry, and her eyes began watering, too. She had no idea how much she'd empathize with LaShaun's pain.

LaShaun dried her tears and swung her chair back around. "Please accept my apologies," she muttered, "I know how unprofessional this must seem."

"Not at all. Is there anything I can do for you? Can I get you anything?"

LaShaun clasped her hands and placed them beneath her chin.

"I'll appreciate it if you keep me posted on any updates until we can figure this thing out."

"Yes, ma'am. I will."

"Good. You're excused now." When Karisma stood, LaShaun got up from her desk and entered her bathroom.

Dejected that she'd been abruptly dismissed by her boss once again, Karisma dropped her head and rushed to the bathroom to calm her nerves. *You've done nothing wrong. He's done nothing wrong. Everything is okay.* She paced back and forth in front of the stalls. She stopped when the door opened.

Ms. Smith entered the restroom, so Karisma quickly moved to the sink to wash her hands.

"Is everything okay? Ms. Smith's piercing eyes lasered in on Karisma.

"Yes, Ma'am, it is." Karisma grabbed a paper towel and dried her hands.

"The officer said you might have information about the deacon's case. Is that true?" She stood near Karisma.

"No. I don't know anything other than what I've heard on the internet."

"I don't have to tell you how important this case is to Lady Delaney, do I?"

Is she trying to intimidate me? Karisma stepped back. "Like I told the officer, I wasn't near the hotel that night or any other night. Hopefully, they find the person they're looking for, but it isn't me."

Ms. Smith looked at Karisma as if the word liar was written across her forehead. "Umm hmm," she said slowly. "I pray you're being truthful." She then turned to enter a stall. Karisma hurriedly went to the conference room.

At the end of her shift, she hightailed out of the office, heading to her aunt's house, which was three blocks from the church. She needed Rod to tell her what was going on, especially now that she'd been dragged into a murder investigation.

But when she arrived, Rod was nowhere to be found.

LaShaun could sense Karisma knew more than what she admitted. There was no doubt in her mind. She wanted to press her for more information, but if she wanted to avoid alarming Karisma, the timing wasn't right. She grabbed a prepaid cell from her laptop case and dialed Charlotte to inform her of the latest developments.

"I don't think it's a coincidence her car was seen in the hotel's vicinity," LaShaun added after she'd told her everything. "You need to determine what she knows."

"I'm on it," Charlotte said when LaShaun finished. These three words should've lifted LaShaun's burdens, but they could mean anything with Charlotte. LaShaun typically gave her free reign to put out fires, but she was going to hold her on a tight leash with this case.

"Just find out what she knows," LaShaun instructed. "Then report back to me. I'll decide what action needs to be taken."

"Sure thing, *boss*," Charlotte responded sarcastically. On another note, the virus is spreading faster than anyone expected so our attorney is listening to Dr. Fauci and the Center for Disease control. He suggests we shut down operations in New York and Atlanta since it's highly contagious and has no cure. It's now expected to kill millions."

"Why those locations?"

"Were you not listening? It's deadly and extremely contagious. It's airborne, and if you get too close to someone who has it, or touches surfaces that have been infected, you will catch it. The

Atlanta and New York airports have been tagged as hotspots for the virus, particularly for people flying in from out of the country. Our international and national clientele makes us vulnerable."

"Let's see what we can find out from our friends on The Hill. If all this is true, they'll let us know. Of all people, they don't want our operations to cease."

Charlotte laughed. "I don't think a deadly virus will shut us down, but we don't need to put our girls at risk. Even if we keep operating, we may have to modify things slightly."

LaShaun knew many girls depended on the boutique for tuition, housing, healthcare, etc., and they would continue to get paid. Her concern, however, was on Karisma. If she was connected in any way to Claudia, there's a strong possibility she knows about the inner workings of Sweet Dreams Boutique. And information in the wrong hands was like a ticking time bomb; it could blow LaShaun's world to pieces at any time.

Chapter Seven
THE DEVIL'S PLAYGROUND

The praise team was singing as LaShaun quietly slipped inside the church, hustling past the sanctuary where the congregants were gathered for Bible study. She loved praise and worship. Sometimes, the songs ministered to her in a way that the Word couldn't, penetrating her mind the same way worship penetrated her heart. But she couldn't hang around listening; she had work to do.

LaShaun headed straight to Langston's office, hoping to lay her head on his chest and feel his arms wrapped around her. That was her safe place.

When she arrived at her husband's door, an armor bearer was on post.

"Hi, Edgar! She reached out to hug him.

"Hi, First Lady," he responded awkwardly as he returned her hug. He continued to stand in front of Langston's door, preventing her from entering. She was taken aback by his odd behavior.

"Is Langston in a meeting? Can I go in?"

"I'm sorry, First Lady. But Pastor asked that he not be disturbed... by anyone." He glanced at her apologetically.

LaShaun was deeply disturbed. "Since when did I become just anyone?" She put her hands on her hips and stared at him defiantly.

"Please First Lady," Edgar pleaded. "I'm just following orders. I don't mean any disrespect to you. You know I would let you in if I could."

LaShaun calmed down. "You're right, Edgar. I apologize. I will talk to him after study," she said reluctantly. He thanked her for understanding, and she headed to the sanctuary. Her concern rose with each step she took.

What is so important that I can't go into his office? Did something happen that I don't know about?

It had been a long time since LaShaun walked down the center aisle of the sanctuary like the rest of the congregation. She normally entered from the side door, with Langston. And she was used to people staring at her, but the whispers that pricked her ears as she forced her feet to move indicated something serious was going on. *Do they know something I don't?* Maintaining her composure, she smiled and strolled confidently as she made her way to the front pew.

When she settled in her seat, LaShaun was careful to acknowledge gawkers with a wave and air kiss. Some waved back, others turned their heads in the opposite direction. She opened her Bible and kept her eyes glued to the pages, not even participating in praise and worship.

Maybe I'm being paranoid, but something is off. She'd stopped caring what people thought about her long ago, but with everything going on, her antennas were up. She raised her head as Langston entered the sanctuary. The congregation clapped as he strolled to the podium and had the praise team take their seats. He didn't even turn his head LaShaun's way; she was perturbed by his snub.

I'm here every Wednesday night and every Sunday morning. I bend over backward for this ministry and you. How dare you ignore me!

As agitated as she was, LaShaun fought her feelings and tried to show support, like a *good* Christian wife. She refused to show any cracks in her armor. Church folk loved when drama hit the pastor's house. Sure, they loved Langston. But a little drama kept him humble and gave them license to continue their mess.

Langston trudged through his lesson with little fanfare or emotion, and LaShaun felt something brewing in the atmosphere. As soon as he concluded his message, he left the sanctuary. LaShaun rose to go to his office to address his demeanor, but she was cornered by a church member.

"Hey First Lady," Isabelle Taylor cackled as she placed an arm around LaShaun's neck and kissed her cheek. Her breath smelled like hot garbage, and fakeness oozed like poison from her abnormally shaped chafed lips.

Sister Isa-Hell (as LaShaun called her in private), got on her last nerve but LaShaun strived to be longsuffering and kind. In as pleasant a voice as she could muster, she responded. "Hi, Sister Isabelle. How are you?"

"I was doing fine until one of these gossiping Jezebels brought some news to me, and my spirit told me I had to come to you. You know there's no way I'm letting *uncurbstantiated* rumors fly around behind your back."

You're an uncurbstantiated lie. Without a word, LaShaun smiled, grappling to understand how someone so old could be so messy. Sister Isabelle's idea of looking out for folks was dishing out what she'd heard because she *hated gossip* so much. Negative news was like a juicy truffle to her-it was obvious she couldn't wait until LaShaun had a taste. Feigning distress, she closed her eyes, shook her head, then looked towards Heaven.

"Now, I don't want to tell you dis First Lady because I don't *like* to speak evil of the dead," Sister Isabelle lowered her voice with a callous grin, "but word on the streets is Deacon Thomas was with a prostitute when he had that heart att---."

"Sister Isabelle, just take it to the Lord in prayer," LaShaun interrupted, "we are not to concern ourselves with what's happening *in the streets*."

"Then let me tell you what's going on in the church." Sister Isabelle quickly scanned the vicinity to make sure everyone within earshot could hear her. "Word is, the girl he was with is a member of your sorority." Sister Isabelle slapped the back of LaShaun's hand and poked her lips out.

LaShaun snatched her Bible and purse from the pew. "I will not entertain these lies, Sister Isabelle. You have a good night."

"I don't think you get it, First Lady. Or should I call you, *Madame?*" Sister Isabelle unleashed a sinister grin. "The rumor around here is, you're pimping out that little girl and some of your other sorority sisters. They say that baby works for you." Sister Isabelle cocked her head, pointing at LaShaun while she clucked her tongue on the roof of her mouth.

LaShaun heard others snickering in the background. She wanted to slap the taste out of the old woman's mouth and drag her down the aisle by her matted, dusty wig. But by the strength of God alone, she turned around and stormed off.

"The Bible warns us to beware of lying tongues, Sister Isabelle," LaShaun called over her shoulder. "I would hate for you to get caught up in church gossip and displease the Lord."

Sister Isabelle screeched, stopping LaShaun in her tracks to face her again. "That's why I'm bringing this to you. I've heard your boutique is the devil's playground, and I don't want nobody *scantilizing* you like that. I just want you to set the record straight. Of course, as long as what they're saying isn't true."

LaShaun was livid. "Get thee behind me, Satan," she uttered through gritted teeth before spinning on her heels to strut out of the sanctuary with as much dignity as she could, the same way she strutted in. *Please don't let me beat this old biddy in this sanctuary.*

"First Lady, come back. What I say?" Sister Isabelle called as LaShaun bolted through the vestibule doors.

LaShaun fumed. Langston ignored her throughout his lesson and left the sanctuary without so much as a glance in her direction. Sure, his silence hurt, but it didn't hurt worse than him shunning her publicly.

He treated her like she was nothing more than a side chick, one he could not acknowledge for fear it would cause the congregation to question his fidelity. Now that he'd disrespected her publicly, members of the congregation were free to do the same. He put the knife in her back; Sister Isabelle twisted it.

Tears flowed down LaShaun's face in anger. When she pulled into the garage and cut the engine, she laid her head on the steering wheel and bawled. She felt alone and vulnerable. She'd always been able to depend on Langston's wisdom and comfort when she was overwhelmed. Now, she felt she had no one.

LaShaun entered her home and headed straight to the shower. As she let the warm water massage the back of her neck, she thought about all the women Sweet Dreams Boutique empowered, and that gave her strength. They were now in a position to control their destinies.

These ladies support their families, sit on high-powered boards, fund summer camps for impoverished youth, and so much more. They've always been the CEO of their bodies, with absolute control over how they want to profit from them. Their choice? To boss up for themselves instead of working like dogs for someone else. How they made their living was no one's business.

Chapter Eight
THE ENEMY'S SNARE

After LaShaun finished showering, she was busy oiling her body when she looked at the clock perched on her nightstand. It was ten thirty, and Langston still hadn't come home. It was typical for him to remain at the church talking to his deacons after Bible study; however, he usually made it home at a decent hour.

She picked up her phone to check for missed calls. Not a peep from Langston, just a missed call from Charlotte. A knot formed in the pit of her stomach. *Is he okay? Has he been hurt?*

Although LaShaun wasn't mentally prepared for a fight, she had to call and check on him. It wasn't like him to leave her home alone this late at night. She dialed his number, and it went straight to voicemail. *God, please let him be okay,* she prayed.

Fifteen minutes later, she found herself dialing him again. Straight to voicemail. Without thinking, she called Deacon Thomas's number.

You've reached Deacon Thomas. I am not available to take your call. Please leave a message, and I will get back to you short-.

LaShaun had forgotten the first person she usually turned to when she was unable to reach Langston was gone. She grabbed her pillow, curled up in a ball, and cried.

She cried for Deacon Thomas, her marriage, and all the people who would be ruined if an investigation revealed their involvement in Sweet Dreams. *Why did he have to die in such a scandalous way?*

Her cell buzzed. It was a message from Langston. She swiped the screen.

I need time to think, so I'm heading to the Ritz. Will be home tomorrow. Make sure all the doors are locked. Ttyl.

Talk to you later. Are you kidding me? Is that what we're doing now? LaShaun's sadness turned to scorn. She dialed Langston's number again and, again, he sent her straight to voicemail. She threw the phone against the wall with all the strength she had. "This man won't even answer my calls," she screamed, "how dare he!"

The phone buzzed, and LaShaun scrambled across the bed for it, thinking Langston had come to his senses. It was Charlotte. "Hello," she grumbled.

"Hey hon," Charlotte chirped in her happy-go-lucky tone. "What's up, girl?"

"Are you alright? Sounds like you've been crying."

LaShaun cleared her raspy throat. "I'm fine. Probably catching a cold." Charlotte was always predicting the demise of her and Langston's marriage, so LaShaun was careful how much she let her know.

"You need to take care of yourself. Now is not the time to be getting sick."

LaShaun ignored her friend's concern. "Why are you calling so late? You know I don't talk on the phone when Langston's home."

"Are you sure he's home? I'm told he just checked in at the Ritz."

LaShaun held back a curse. She'd forgotten they had a girl at the front desk of all the major hotels.

"Why is he at the hotel?" Charlotte asked.

"He's upset by everything that's in the media, I suppose." LaShaun rolled her eyes.

"You didn't tell him they were lies?"

"I haven't spoken with him. I didn't get a chance to see him before Bible study, and I came straight home afterward." She scrolled through the messages on her phone, half listening to Charlotte.

"That's cold."

"He just needs time to process everything. It's all over the news." She scrolled through her messages and deleted the ones she no longer needed. Some as old as three months ago.

"Don't worry - it's all speculation. Everyone has a theory. No one has facts. So, deny, deny, deny."

"You're suggesting I continue to lie to him?"

"I shouldn't have to suggest it. You should know what to do. This is not your first rodeo."

"I'm in a no-win situation. If I tell him the truth, I risk bringing harm to you and the girls. If I continue lying, I'll drive a gulf between him and me."

"You know you can't confess to Langston, right?" It was more a command than a question.

"Of course. But lying to him isn't right."

"I know it isn't, but don't lose your mind. I already have someone working to move the heat away from us."

"Who? And what are they going to do? I haven't authorized anything."

"Don't worry about that. I'm taking the lead on this one. Just keep your cool and know that it's being handled." Following a brief pause, Charlotte added, "I called our distinguished gentleman on The Hill. He's confirmed the virus is real, and there are positive cases in the states."

"Are you sure? Why haven't we heard anything from the president?"

"What do you want him to say?" Charlotte launched into a sarcastic, presidential voice. "Hey, everybody! The virus is here, it's the biggest virus we've ever seen, a really bad virus but nobody can kill a virus better than me. I will kill the virus. Don't believe fake news."

LaShaun smirked. "Hee, hee, heifer. You just don't like him because you listen to *fake news*."

"It's not that I don't like him; it's the incompetent way he's managing - no, mismanaging our country. The man is a poster child for racism, sexism, and many other isms. He doesn't have the country's best interest on his agenda and was put in office to return America to the good ol' boys, by any means necessary."

LaShaun refused to argue politics with Charlotte. They'd been down this road before, and it would not end well. "The president is the least of my worries," she sighed. "What are we going to do about our situation?"

"As I said, it's being handled. I'm not telling you so you can always have plausible deniability."

"I'm not sure that's possible. I'm an equal partner and equally liable for whatever happens."

"Nothing will happen. We're tying up loose ends, that's all."

LaShaun slid down and laid her head on her pillow. "Well, we'll leave it at that. I'm drained. I'll talk to you tomorrow."

"Ok. Try to get some sleep."

"I will. Bye." They disconnected the call and LaShaun went to bed, falling asleep immediately.

The next morning, LaShaun fixed herself a cup of coffee and made a bagel, with strawberry cream cheese. She'd given Rosa the week off to visit her daughter, who'd given birth to her first grandchild.

While drinking the coffee, she paced in front of the living room's bay window, still waiting for Langston to come back home. She was still upset by the way he treated her during Bible Study, then staying at the hotel the night before.

Up until now, forgiving each other quickly had been the hallmark of their relationship. And although he disregarded her feelings and safety last night, LaShaun held onto the love she knew he had for her. But that didn't mean the way he disrespected her didn't cut to the core.

She'd vowed to never be at the mercy of anyone, and now here she was. Her eyes were bloodshot and swollen from crying, her stomach in perpetual knots, and forming a complete thought was impossible at this point. She was a wreck.

Charlotte called as LaShaun was placing her mug in the sink.

"Hello?" LaShaun walked to her bedroom and reclined on her chaise lounge.

"Hey, girl. Is Langston home yet?"

"Not yet." LaShaun sighed.

"Good. I have some news for you."

"What is it?" LaShaun asked unfazed.

"I spoke to Cruz to see if he could give me an update on the investigation."

"Stop spoon-feeding me," LaShaun said irritably. "What did he say?"

Charlotte paused before answering. "Now don't get alarmed, but they were able to get a copy of security footage from the hospital, and it shows you were the last person in his room before the nurse found him unresponsive."

"What!!!" LaShaun jumped up and paced the floor.

"Don't have a conniption! That doesn't prove you killed him. But, unfortunately, you're now a person of interest."

LaShaun's heart raced. "You've got to be kidding me," she said as she sat on her bed. "I can't believe this is happening."

"It's just a bump in the road. We'll get through this. According to Cruz, about six o'clock this morning, the lead detective tried to obtain a search warrant to search the boutique and your home, but Judge Bennett denied their request, citing a failure to show probable cause."

LaShaun couldn't speak. She felt lightheaded. She placed her head between her legs and took deep breaths in and out until she felt normal again. Charlotte could hear her heavy breathing and stopped talking.

"Anything else?" she asked after she calmed down.

"I called Judge Bennett, and he said that Deacon Thomas's credit card statement and your appearance in his hospital room are not enough to rise to reasonable suspicion that you may have committed a crime."

"Thank God," LaShaun stressed. She and Langston were generous donors to the judge's election campaigns and his summer camp for at-risk youth. More compelling was the fact the judge was a regular patron of the boutique. Therefore, she felt safe in saying there was no way he was going to pave the way for anything that could point back to him.

Once again, she was spared from the enemy's snare.

Chapter Nine
THE SWEETNESS OF WINE

Queen Heir Purse Boutique was draining Heiress dry. She'd gone to the Chamber of Commerce, local fairs, and the internet to promote her business. She was in the store from sunup to sundown, praying customers into the shop. She even passed out flyers to customers going to neighboring businesses, promising a twenty-five percent discount off their total, all to no avail.

In January, business was booming. Purses were flying off the shelves, and Heiress had made a sizable profit. In anticipation of Valentine's Day, she placed a huge order to replenish her inventory. By April, the United States was in a state of emergency due to the Coronavirus, and businesses were closing.

Heiress was grateful if she sold one or two purses a week. The mayor refused to mandate store closures, but it didn't matter. Potential customers were so afraid of the virus they stayed at home voluntarily.

Heiress's mother believed with every bone in her body that God had sent the virus as a plague on our country as He did in the book of Exodus. And every day, she called Heiress to make sure she was truly saved. Heiress was awaiting the day when her mother would instruct her to kill a lamb and spread its blood on her doorposts.

Heiress was busy dusting the purse case when the store's doorbell chimed. Hearing the infrequent sound brought a smile to her face. She scurried behind the counter to return the duster and check her appearance. "If looks could sell, I'd never go broke," she affirmed under her breath and bolted to the door. To her dismay, it wasn't a customer who was waiting for her. It was Detective Cruz.

"It's okay, I won't bite." He flashed an easy grin. Blushing, Heiress opened the door wider and let him in. He was looking better today than he did during his last visit a month ago when he was investigating LaShaun. Following behind him as he headed towards her checkout counter, Heiress asked, "To what do I owe the pleasure, Detective Cruz?"

Stopping mid-stride and turning around, he flashed his seductive smile as Heiress accidentally ran into his chest and jumped back.

He held up both hands. "Well, I had some business nearby, and decided to stop by for a visit." He hid the fact Charlotte ordered him to seduce her so he could find out everything she knew about the boutique's inner workings.

Maneuvering around the handsome man, Heiress eased behind the counter and jammed a hand on her hip. "You're outside of your jurisdiction, aren't you?"

He openly scanned her body, placed his hands on the counter, and leaned close to Heiress. "I could have sent someone else to speak to you, but why would I deny myself the pleasure of those beautiful hazel eyes and your.... other assets?"

Heiress's heart skipped a beat; she felt flushed. She picked up the bottle of water from under the counter, opened it, and gulped. "So, what can I do for you again?"

Detective Cruz straightened up. "Have you spoken with LaShaun Delaney since my last visit?"

She shifted on one leg. "It's been a minute. Why are you still asking about her?"

"I'm still tying up loose ends."

"Why?" she asked defensively. "The deacon's family is grasping at straws. His death had nothing to do with foul play. In their grief they just want someone to blame."

"They were right to request an autopsy. The man was scheduled to be released from the hospital the next day."

"Are you saying he was murdered?"

Without responding, he turned and strolled over to the display case. "Why do women spend such an obscene amount of money on purses?" he asked, trying to divert her attention.

Her hands began sweating. *Does he think I wanted to kill him or that I know who killed him? Is he trying to tie me to it and his little flirtation is a ruse to catch me off guard? Do I need a lawyer?*

Heiress didn't realize she asked the last question aloud until Vic responded, "Why would you need a lawyer?"

Flustered, Heiress blew out a long breath and slapped her forehead. "You're interrogating me, so obviously you think I'm involved in his death. I just want to make sure that what I say isn't used against me." Her voice quivered beneath a trail of tears.

Vic walked behind the counter and pulled Heiress into his arms.

Holding her close to his chest, he rubbed his hands up and down her back. His actions crossed the line, but apparently, he didn't care. "I don't think you're involved," he whispered.

Heiress lifted her head, staring into his eyes. Feeling safe with him, she backed away and walked over to the loveseat in the sitting area. After cleaning her eyes with a tissue to remove her smudged eyeliner, Heiress invited him to join her. He took a seat in one of the two rose-colored armchairs that faced the lilac loveseat, adorned with a cream throw.

"So you're a Work of Art?" he smiled.

"Was it the lilac and rose that blew my cover?" she joked. Lilac and Rose were her sorority colors.

"Something like that." He fiddled with a squishy stress relief ball that was placed on the round leather ottoman centered between the sofa and chairs.

"Seriously. Who would want to kill the deacon?" Heiress asked innocently.

"That's the million-dollar question."

"How did he die?"

"We're still awaiting the autopsy."

Trying to clear her mind of negative thoughts, Heiress reached over to the coffee table and poured herself a glass of wine. She sniffed the wine before taking a sip, breasts slowly rising as she inhaled.

She noticed how Detective Cruz couldn't take his eyes off her as she swirled the liquid in her glass and placed it to her lips. She grew warmer as she watched him watching her.

Over the next hour, Heiress and Vic flirted as they got to know each other better. She'd spent most days with a headache and was on pins and needles wondering whether her business would survive from one month to the next, but he was a welcome respite from her troubles.

Although she'd been celibate for a year, he awakened every desire she'd tried so hard to suppress. She didn't want to renege on her vow to God, but she needed relief from all the pressure. And she began to envision herself seducing him.

As if reading her mind, he asked, "Is there anything I can do for you...*Heiress*?"

She melted at the way he said *Heiress* and pondered her next move. *He wants me just as much as I want him. Why else has he stayed?* "What do you want to do for me?" she asked as she slowly traced the rim of her glass.

His smoldering eyes answered her, and she used her index finger to beckon him to come closer. He moved from the chair to the loveseat. When he sat, she closed the gap between them. As he stared lustfully, she leaned forward and used her tongue to caress his bottom lip.

He tried to restrain himself, then reached around and grabbed her lower back, pulling her even closer. Taking control, he slid his tongue into her mouth. She moaned with pleasure as their tongues intertwined. The sweetness of wine removed all inhibitions.

Thoroughly enraptured, Vic's hand moved from Heiress's back to her breast. As his thumb lightly caressed her nipple, she knew they'd reached the point of no return. Her tongue tasted the salty flesh on his neck as his hand caressed the skin between her thighs. As he released a slight whimper, she gently pushed him onto his back.

Still wearing her red bottom heels, she lifted her dress over her head, threw it on the floor, and straddled him. He reached behind her to unhook her bra. Taking her hardened areola in his mouth, he massaged it ever so slightly. Other parts of her body responded as sexual electricity rushed through her.

Lifting her, he flipped her onto her back. She fought her conscience as Vic moved his pelvic area in and out in a slow, rhythmic motion.

We need to stop. No, I need this release. I don't know this man. What am I doing? But I haven't felt this good in a long time. I can't stop.

Pretty soon, Vic invaded Heiress's thoughts. "Do you want me to stop?"

"No," Heiress whispered. *Lord, please forgive me.* She was on the brink of ecstasy, and Vic still had his pants on. She hadn't felt this sensual in a long time and didn't want it to end.

With all the urgency of a snail, he pulled down his slacks and put on protection. Then, he gave Heiress a long, impassioned kiss before giving her what she'd been yearning for since he walked in the door. And she enjoyed every. single. fascinating. moment.

Chapter Ten
A LONG TIME COMING

Karisma awakened to the sound of her alarm and an excruciating headache. Detectives had picked her up as she was leaving her aunt's home and she'd been interrogated for several hours regarding Deacon Thomas's murder.

She'd cried herself to sleep last night and wanted to stay curled up in her warm cozy bed the rest of the day, but she couldn't. She had a test to take, and she could hear her mother saying, *Get up girl. The world is no place for a weak black woman.*

Her mother was right - the world wouldn't stop while Karisma found the strength to get herself together. She had to move right along with it or die trying.

Begrudgingly, she dragged herself from the bed and made her

way to the shower. She relaxed under the pressure of the steaming water with her eyes closed as the water cascaded from her head to her feet.

The steady stream rained down on her like a liquid salve and calmed her as she permitted herself to shed tears over her predicament. She'd overcome every obstacle that tried to derail her, and this time would be no different. Jail was not on her vision board, and the police would not hijack her freedom.

On the way to class, her mother called. She wasn't in a state of mind to discuss last night's harrowing events, so she sent her straight to voicemail. If she answered, her mother would immediately detect something was wrong, and the barrage of questions would begin. Since she didn't want to answer any questions until she spoke with her cousin Rod, she'd have to call her back. As she drove the twenty minutes to campus, she replayed last night's interrogation.

After an hour of asking the same question, the investigator tried a different one. "Ms. Stanley, a confidential informant called the *CrimeSpotters* tip line and informed us you were the person on the surveillance video entering the white Honda Accord on December 19, 2019. Is that true?"

"No," she answered.

"Where were you on the 19th, Ms. Stanley?"

"Let me go or let me call my lawyer," she squeaked. "I don't know where the hotel is, I was not in its vicinity, and I didn't know the man who died. You're holding me for no reason, and I want my one phone call."

"You're not under arrest, so you are not entitled to a phone call."

"Then release me so I can go home."

"There's no need to be uncooperative if you have nothing to hide."

Karisma was well aware she was being filmed. "Don't try to tag me as uncooperative. You wake me out of my sleep and haul me down here at an indecent hour, put me under bright florescent lights, stall for at least an hour, offer me nothing more than a sip of tepid metallic-tasting water, badger me, *and* call me a murderer. Yet, you expect me to respond pleasantly to your never-ending questions. I have been more than cooperative. So, let me go or let me call my lawyer."

"We're only trying to get justice for the family."

Carefully enunciating every word, Karisma stated, "I want my lawyer."

"Take a look at this picture again. If you can help us identi-"

"I want my lawyer!" She glared at the lead detective and crossed her arms. "Now."

The detective looked at the darkened observation window behind Karisma, nodding his head as if giving someone a signal. "Sit tight," he instructed and left the room. Thirty minutes later, a different police officer came in and told Karisma she was free to go.

He escorted her to the revolving door leading outside, and she mused at how easily the same door led to freedom and bondage simultaneously. Her mother and father were waiting for her when she exited the building. She didn't feel like talking, and they didn't ask any questions. They drove home in silence, and she went straight to bed.

After her test, Karisma drove to DMI. Ms. Smith wasn't at her desk when she arrived, so she knocked on LaShaun's door. Even though her Tesla was in her designated parking space, the outer door leading to her office suite was locked. When she turned to leave, the door opened.

LaShaun was disheveled. Her mascara was smeared, her hair was in disarray, and she had dried mucus on her nose. She raked a hand through her wild hair as if that would fix things. "I thought you weren't coming in today," she murmured.

"I wasn't supposed to, but I wanted to tell you what happened to me last night," Karisma said. "It can wait, though. Are you okay? Can I do anything for you?"

"It's sweet of you to ask, but no. I'm just not feeling well." LaShaun did her best to smooth her hair, but it didn't work. "What is it you want to discuss?"

Karisma blinked twice when LaShaun wiped her nose with the back of her hand. "I can come back when you're feeling better," she said. "Are you sure you even need to be here?"

Karisma hated seeing LaShaun this way. She always appeared so strong on television, but now she was falling apart. Just yesterday, an *Atlanta Metro Times* reporter accosted her in the parking lot with a barrage of questions about the seedy nature of Sweet Dreams Boutique and allegations of sex trafficking AU students. From the looks of things, everything was taking a toll on her.

"You came to see me, and I would hate for it to be in vain," LaShaun said. "Let me freshen up a bit, and we'll talk." LaShaun welcomed the distraction, and she was curious about the reason for Karisma's visit on her off day.

It was a while before LaShaun reemerged from the bathroom with a clean face and her hair intact. She took a seat at her desk and smiled.

"So, what can I do for you, Karisma?"

"Um...I was taken to the police station last night to be interrogated about Deacon Thomas's death," Karisma answered nervously. "I thought you'd want to know."

"What? Are you serious?"

"Unfortunately, yes. They still believe my car is the white Honda that was captured on camera near the time of the deacon's death, and now someone has called the tipline and told them I was the person entering the car, not driving it."

"That must have been horrible for you," LaShaun said. "What did you tell them?"

"The same thing I've been saying since day one. That my car was stolen, and I had nothing to do with any of this."

LaShaun looked pensive. "Hmmm. That should be the end of it. I'm sure they won't bother you anymore. If they had evidence to the contrary, they wouldn't have released you."

"I won't hold my breath," Karisma said, defeated. "I keep getting dragged into this case somehow."

LaShaun was genuinely sorry that she was involved. She didn't say it, but she believed Charlotte may be the anonymous tipper. She was the only person LaShaun knew with the motive and gall to point the finger at an innocent child.

LaShaun rose and sat on the front edge of her desk, closer to Karisma. "If there's anything I can do to make things easier for you, please let me know. You can take some time off if needed."

"No, there's no need for that. I took my last test today, and classes are being conducted online for the remainder of this semester. That will provide me with a much-needed break."

"That's good to hear. Let me know if you change your mind."

Karisma got up from her seat and thanked her. Then LaShaun

walked her to the door. Karisma reminded Lashaun of herself. Striving to project a pillar of strength when she could crumble at any moment. And she prayed Karisma was truthful with her. For, she knew if Charlotte was the person who gave the tip to the police, Karisma's troubles were just beginning.

Chapter Eleven

LORD, GUIDE MY TONGUE

LaShaun was at the kitchen counter eating oatmeal with slithered almonds, brown sugar, and cranberries when she heard the garage door rising. Langston was home. He'd stayed away two nights and had not been at DMI when LaShaun was there. It had been hard for her to go to the office herself, but she believed her absence would cause the members to believe everything said about her in the media. And she wouldn't give them the satisfaction of thinking she was tucking her tail and hiding.

She'd been anxiously awaiting Langston's return, but now her heart raced at the thought of the conversation she knew would take place. To gather herself, she sprinted to her bathroom before he entered the house. As she closed the door and locked it, she quickly prayed.

Dear Lord, you said I could come boldly before your throne God, and I am following your Word. Please have mercy on me, Father. Please forgive my sins and cover me as the investigation into Deacon Thomas's death goes forward. Father, please protect Langston and shield him from any personal or ministerial harm. Speak to me and through me as I talk to him, and Lord please guide my tongue. In Jesus's name. Amen.

Langston knocked on the door just as her prayer ended. "I'm home, LaShaun."

His solemn tone said the conversation they were about to have wouldn't be a pleasant one.

"Ok. I'll be out in a second."

"Take your time." He left the bedroom and went into the kitchen.

When she finally emerged from the bathroom, she found him standing in the dining room, peering out the bay window. His hands were in his pockets and tension caused his shoulders to hunch.

She walked across the room and sat at the table. *Don't be adversarial. A soft answer turns away wrath.* "Hi, Langston. I'm glad you decided to come home." *Dang, that didn't come out right.*

When Langston turned to face her, his scowl said everything his mouth did not speak. His eyes twitched as if he was struggling not to lash out.

"I stayed away because I was afraid of what I might say or do," he explained aggressively. "You know I work hard to rule my spirit, but with everything I've been told, it has been difficult. I had to process it and calm down before I spoke with you. I hope you can understand that."

She nodded. "I do, but I still deserve more than what you've given me." Then, stabbing the table with her pointer finger and raising her voice, she continued, "This house has seven bedrooms - you had your choice of any one of them to sleep in if you wanted to get away from me that bad."

Langston gave as good as he got. He walked from the window and stood in front of her. "Don't try to turn this on me. This is about you and your lies! If I'd come home before now, it wouldn't have been good for either of us." His nostrils flared as he glared at her.

"But if you'd come home, you could have told me what upset you, and we could've discussed it. I thought that was how we handled conflict!"

"Are you really sitting there pretending that you don't know?" he asked incredulously. He stormed into the living room. Although LaShaun could still see and hear him clearly, she stomped behind him.

Her voice raised another octave. "How could I know what you heard? I don't read minds, Langston!" LaShaun couldn't reign in her emotions.

"Don't get curt with me and don't play dumb." Langston's eyes burned red with rage. "You know exactly why I want to put my hands around your neck and choke the life out of you right now."

LaShaun's breath stopped for a moment, shocked that Langston had spoken to her so harshly. She wanted to get slick with him but remained quiet.

She went to the beige sofa that sat along the living room wall, placed one leg under the opposite thigh, crossed her arms, and stared at him, trying to keep herself from going off.

Langston dropped his head and pinched the bridge of his nose for several minutes. When he raised his head, he walked over to the chair that faced the sofa and sat down.

"Are you still going to pretend you have *no idea* why I'm upset?"

"How am I supposed to know, Langston? You won't have a real conversation with me."

He shook his head, then spoke slowly and deliberately. "I heard Sweet Dreams Boutique isn't anything more than a front for your sorority's prostitution ring, LaShaun. And you're the ringleader." He stared at her, awaiting a response.

"And you believe that?" She gawked at him like he was crazy.

"So, is everyone who told me about you lying, including the police?"

"I never fathomed you would believe or even suggest I am pimping out my Sorors. And if that's not enough, you take the word of some police officers over your wife? As if they've never lied!"

"Those officers are members of our congregation, LaShaun." Langston shook his head in disbelief. "Anything they've told me is out of respect for us and our relationship. Look me in my eyes and tell me they're deliberately lying on you!"

LaShaun couldn't look at him. "Why should I have to say anything, Langston? When did you start questioning my integrity?" She put on the saddest face she could muster, manipulating him.

The aggression deflated from Langston's voice. "I'm not questioning your integrity. But I do know Charlotte runs the business and you're her partner, which ultimately makes you just as responsible for anything that goes on in that boutique."

Langston slid down in his seat, and his head tilted back as if it were being pulled by strings. LaShaun looked at him in silence. After a few minutes passed, he sat up straight and pointed his body towards LaShaun.

"I don't believe you are the ringleader in a sexual exploitation scheme but, honestly, I can't make myself believe you have no idea that sexual activity isn't taking place. But if you look me in my eyes and tell me right now you were never aware, I will go to my grave defending you."

LaShaun chose her words carefully. "I have a very hard time believing Charlotte is doing something illegal without my knowledge. She wouldn't do that."

Langston steepled his hands and sat still for a moment. Then, he moved to the sofa and grabbed her hands. She looked him in the eye. "Are you sure, baby? You and I both know she'll do anything for a dollar."

"Not if it would put us in jeopardy of going to jail. She's not that hungry for money, and neither am I." She rose from the table and went to the refrigerator, pretending to need a drink. "Would you like anything?"

He shook his head, no. She grabbed a ginger ale and popped the cap. She remained at the kitchen counter so Langston couldn't hear the thumping her heart was doing.

Langston didn't believe LaShaun could knowingly break the law, but he knew Charlotte was capable of anything. He'd never trusted her and didn't understand LaShaun's continued relationship with her. Although they'd been best friends in college, they were going in different directions now.

"Listen, I've been assured that Sweet Dreams Boutique has been on the sheriff's radar for some time. Now, I know you don't want to hear it, but it's highly unlikely the blond-haired, blue-eyed white girl will be the one going to jail when everything goes down. It's going to be you. So, if we want to keep that from happening, we have work to do."

LaShaun slowly raised her bowed head. "We?"

Langston walked over to LaShaun, took the soda can from her, and put it on the counter. Then he wrapped her in his arms. "I would die before I let anything, or anyone, harm you, baby. There is a murder investigation pending, and right now you are a suspect. We can't bury our heads in the sand."

"I knew you wouldn't let me down," she said softly.

Strategizing late into the night, they developed a plan of action. The next morning, they assembled a team consisting of their attorney, agent, and publicist.

After much debate, and against their attorney's advice, it was decided they'd sit down with *WKBX's* Simone Peters, host of *The Last Word*, an award-winning daytime talk show that aired locally. She was so grateful for the exclusive, that she bumped her scheduled guest and interviewed them the very next day.

She allowed them to highlight their close relationship with the deacon and love for his family, as well as the new initiative to rename DMI's life center the *Deacon Archibald Thomas Youth Center*. They highlighted the couple's philanthropy and went into great detail about the hundreds of women LaShaun has mentored and helped graduate college.

The segment ended with Langston praising the police department's handling of the investigation and its attempts to find Deacon Thomas's "gutless killer." Lastly, they vowed to hire their own private investigator who would "work tirelessly to find the perpetrator of such a heinous act upon such a devout man."

Later that night, on channel six's ten o'clock news, LaShaun and Langston watched a recap of their interview. When it ended, the anchorman cut to a remote broadcast. Langston and LaShaun were enraptured as the reporter on the scene spoke into the camera.

"*As a result of the ongoing investigation into the death of Archibald*

Thomas, a resident who was found unresponsive at the Lancaster Hotel on December 18th, and later died at County Memorial Hospital, the police have arrested a suspect."

He pointed to the dorms behind him, and the camera zoomed to a window on the second floor.

"A short while ago, a search warrant was served upon a student residing in Room 204 Plunkett Hall, on the campus of Atlanta University."

The reporter reappeared on screen, reading a paper he held in his hand. "Karisma Stanley, a Junior, has been arrested in connection with the case. We will be following this story and will bring you any future developments."

Langston was dumbfounded, and LaShaun was livid. *I know Charlotte ain't trying to get this young girl caught up. She has lost her devilish mind!*

Chapter Twelve
NO OTHER WAY

LaShaun left her home at six o'clock the next morning and headed to Charlotte's safe house - a luxury cabin in the mountains of North Georgia, nestled behind a grove of maple and oak trees, sitting on seventy-five acres. Trees were beginning to sprout leaves, and other vegetation was coming to life. The grounds were equipped with a helipad, and a personal pilot resided in an adjacent cabin-ensuring the *H160 Airbus was always* ready for takeoff.

Years ago, Charlotte purchased the estate through one of her shell corporations. She'd go to the home to lay low after she'd done something egregious. And LaShaun knew that's where she'd find her.

As she drove the forty-five minutes to the cabin, she tried to figure out what Charlotte was up to. There was no doubt in her mind she was behind Karisma's arrest, but she couldn't figure out why she'd chosen her. She was too far removed from anything related to the boutique, and she had no ties to Deacon Thomas. Charlotte hadn't shared any of her plans with LaShaun, and she was beginning to worry. Especially since she was normally the one who called the shots.

When she reached her destination, she put her car in park, stepped out, and surveyed Charlotte's property. *If things go south, I have nowhere to run. She could bury me here, and I'll never be found.* LaShaun hadn't considered that possibility before today.

She meandered up the steps and stared at the eight-foot steel front door, built to withstand a battering ram. She didn't get the chance to knock before the door flew open, and Charlotte yanked her inside.

"Girl, get in here! Why didn't you tell me you were coming?" Charlotte pulled her into a tight embrace.

"I wanted to surprise you! I would have been here sooner, but traffic was ridiculous." When Charlotte let go, LaShaun slid away from her and entered the home. LaShaun took in the rustic but chic décor as she shuffled over to the gargantuan couch centered in the center of the cabin.

Charlotte sat next to her. "What brings you to my neck of the woods? Is hubby still giving you the silent treatment?"

As if you care. "Langston's not talking much, but he comes home every night. I'm satisfied with that, for now." She felt a cool breeze brush across her arms and felt ill at ease. She looked around to see if anything was amiss.

A smug grin crossed Charlotte's face. "Are you sure about that? When he finds out all the rumors are true, do you think he'll stick by you? He has a lot to lose."

"The only thing he can't stand to lose is me. We'll weather this storm like we did all the others." Her face started to heat up as she angered. She shifted her body, trying to get comfortable.

Charlotte grinned and poked further. "You've never faced a challenge this big, though. As they say, this may be the straw that breaks the camel's back."

It was pointless to get wrangled into a conversation about her and Langston's relationship, so LaShaun dismissed her comment. Instead, she decided to catch Charlotte off guard.

"Help me understand why you decided to put Karisma on the chopping block. With all the prison time she's facing, this girl's life will be ruined, if it isn't already! Surely you can't be that evil."

Charlotte was baffled by her frankness, but she didn't deny the allegation. "It hurt me to do it, but there was no other way."

LaShaun rose from the couch defensively. "There's always another way! You could have let the case die due to a lack of evidence."

Charlotte stood and gestured with her hands as she spoke. "Don't you see? Everything about this case points to Sweet Dreams, and none of this is just going to go away or magically disappear. Especially with the media all over it. All I did was steer the investigation in another direction. I had to keep us safe." She looked at LaShaun with pleading eyes.

"Sure, you might be safe, but everything is blowing up in my face!" LaShaun yelled. "In case you haven't noticed, my title has gone from *first lady* to *pimp*. Meanwhile, no one has even uttered your name!"

"Why should they?" Charlotte spat with venom. "I don't have my face splattered across multiple billboards. I'm not married to the most prominent man on this side of the Mississippi. I know how to be low-key. So don't get snippy with me; thank me. I'm trying to keep your ungrateful behind out of jail."

"At the expense of an innocent young girl. Are you serious?" LaShaun shook her head in disbelief.

"Do you know what would happen if the authorities got too close to the truth? *You* would be behind bars. *Your* life would be over." Charlotte barked. "My way puts the focus on someone other than you. Use your brain, LaShaun." She pecked LaShauns's forehead with her thumb, and LaShaun slapped her hand away.

"You think I want you to save me by sending a child to jail? Are you crazy?"

Charlotte stared at her quizzically. "There's no concrete connection between Karisma and Sir Lancelot. A decent lawyer should have no problem helping that girl beat the charges."

LaShaun sat on the nearest chair and held her head down as she calmed herself. *Lord, please deliver me from evil. I can't do it by myself.*

Charlotte got on her knees in front of LaShaun and grabbed her hands. "This will all blow over soon. You'll see. I had to do it this way. I've been getting calls from our customers, and they don't like the heat that's come over the boutique. So, I had to do something drastic. This way, you won't have to worry about the business, and can focus on your marriage."

"I'm always worried about the business, Char."

Charlotte sat down and leaned back on her hands. Speaking softly, she responded, "Then maybe it's time to let it go. You created a wonderful life for yourself. All I have is the boutique. Let me buy you out so you can put all this behind you. Then, you and Langston can be happy again."

As LaShaun looked into Charlotte's eyes, she received a revelation. Charlotte wasn't trying to take the heat off her. If she were, then someone else would face charges, not her personal assistant.

Charlotte was attempting to steer the heat away from the

boutique while simultaneously putting so much pressure on LaShaun and Langston's relationship, that she would have no choice but to relinquish her interest in the boutique and give Charlotte complete control.

This heifer is trying to stage a coup. Has she forgotten who I am? Let me play along with this little charade.

Feigning interest, LaShaun asked, "How would allowing you to buy *me* out change anything?"

Charlotte didn't answer right away. She put her pointer finger to her lips as if pondering the question. "Well, I haven't thought about it, but if that's something you want to do my lawyer can draw up a proposal."

"You've already talked to him about it?" LaShaun asked nonchalantly.

Charlotte tsked. "No, why would I?" She rose from the floor. "You hungry?"

"No, I'm good." LaShaun walked over to the kitchen. Charlotte removed bottled water from the refrigerator.

"Do you think that's something you want to do?" Charlotte drank water.

"I don't know. I'll look at your proposal, though. If the price is right..." She hunched her shoulders. "On another note, how did you frame Karisma?"

"Don't worry about the weeds. The less you know, the better."

"I hear you, but I don't want to be in the dark, Char. This impacts me too much."

"It does, but I have everything under control. Haven't I always taken care of you?"

But you didn't want my business then. Now, you do. "Yes, you have, and I appreciate it. But I want to be more hands-on with this mission."

LaShaun studied Charlotte as she grabbed an apple from the bowl on her bamboo island and began slicing it. "There's nothing to do now. The case has to run its course." She put a slice in her mouth with the tip of the knife. As she chewed, she added, "But, trust me. Karisma won't be convicted of anything. I promise you that."

LaShaun felt a chill travel through her body, and she shivered.

"Are you cold," Charlotte asked.

Briskly, LaShaun rubbed both arms. "It's a little chilly. But no worries." Her phone rang.

"Hello?" It was Ms. Smith.

"I just received the call. The Arraignment is at two, and the bond hearing will be immediately thereafter."

LaShaun glanced at Charlotte, who was chopping her apple slices into bite-size pieces. "Ok. I'll be there. Did you make the transfer?"

"Don't I always," Ms. Smith declared.

LaShaun smiled. "Thank you. I'll see you soon." She pressed the END button and walked to the couch to get her purse. "I gotta go. Char. Something important came up."

"You seem anxious. Is everything okay?" Charlotte followed her to the door.

"It's an issue at DMI. Nothing too major." When LaShaun opened the door, she turned to face Charlotte, who poked out her lips, pretending to pout.

LaShaun chuckled. "Don't be mad. I'll call you later." She blew a kiss at her, then shut the door.

As she trotted down the steps, Charlotte opened the door and yelled, "Don't worry about the boutique…I have it under control!"

Not for long, my friend…Not for long, LaShaun thought as she waved, entered her vehicle, and drove off.

Chapter Thirteen
DISHONOR

Dressed in a red silk pajama short set, Karisma had been studying for her political science exam when she heard a thunderous knock at her door. "This is Officer Johnson of the AU Safety Department; open up!"

"Coming," Karisma shouted grumpily. She scrambled to slip on an oversized AU sweatshirt to cover herself, then swung the door open. Standing before her were six uniformed officers, poised to take the unarmed girl down if necessary. "Ca...can I help you?" she stuttered.

"Are you Karisma Stanley?" one of the officers asked gruffly.

Karisma's heart dropped, and her throat went dry. "Yes sir."

"I'm Chief Detective Killebrew." The man held up his badge. "We have a warrant to search your belongings." He shoved a folded piece of paper at her. She read it, but didn't know if it was legit; however, she was too afraid to contest it, so she stepped back to let them enter. A herd of officers filled the room, pushing her aside.

Teary-eyed and trembling with fear, she asked, "Can I get my phone to call my mother?"

A young officer who looked no more than twenty answered, "Sorry, Ma'am, but you'll have to leave the room. We can't allow you to take any of your belongings." He gently took her by the arms and escorted her out of the room.

Her trepidation quickly turned to humiliation as other students flooded the hallway, cell phones in hand, recording every detail. Karisma kept her head down to avoid looking into the lens aimed in her direction.

The officer guarded her like the queen's sentry. One false move and he'd pounce.

Ten minutes later, Detective Killebrew exited the room with a look of disgust. "Face the wall and put your hands behind your back," he commanded.

Karisma's knees buckled, and the young officer grabbed her. "Why?" she managed to croak, "I haven't done anything! Please let me call my mom!"

Ignoring her pleas, the detective spun her around, grabbed her wrists, and forced on the handcuffs.

"Nooo!" Karisma groaned, tears streaming down her face. She tried to turn around as she exclaimed, "I'm telling you... I haven't done any-"

Manhandling her, the detective abruptly used his knee to pin her against the wall as he recited, "You have the right to remain silent. Anything you say can and will be used against you in a court of law. You have the right to an attorney. If you cannot afford an attorney, one will be appointed to represent you."

"Represent me for what?" Karisma wailed. "Why are you arresting me?" She tried wriggling away from Officer Killibrew, but his grip on her was too strong, and he dragged her down the crowded hallway.

"Please find Cailyn and tell her to call my mom!" Karisma yelled to Carson, their friend who lived two doors from her.

"I will," Carson yelled behind her. "Hang in there, girl!"

Karisma hung her head in shame as she was perp-walked out of the building. Students littered the lawn, and reporters were all around her, snapping pictures and throwing out questions to her and the officers.

All Karisma could focus on was having to tell her mom she'd been arrested. She knew it'd be hell and would rather hang a millstone around her neck and be drowned in a lake than deliver the news to her.

Although she's innocent, Deyja would consider the dishonor Karisma brought upon her good name an unpardonable sin.

Karisma jammed her eyes shut as she was placed in the back seat of the patrol car. She was desperate to speak to God, but it dawned on her she had no idea how to pray. Nevertheless, she said what was in her heart.

"God, please help me," she whispered. She didn't know if the short plea was enough, but for now, it would have to do.

Karisma laid her head on the cold steel table, struggling to find relief for the debilitating headache hammering at her skull.

"We know you had a good reason for killing Mr. Thomas and we want to help you. The sooner you cooperate with us, the better off you'll be," the detective said.

Karisma refused to look at the detective. "You're already convinced of my guilt. Otherwise, you wouldn't have arrested me in such a degrading way. I want a lawyer."

Like magic, the door to the room swung open, and a burly cop barreled inside. An equally intimidating figure followed.

"I'm Ms. Stanley's lawyer," the man's heavy voice boomed. "This interrogation is over." Karisma raised her head and looked at the attorney. He had the same build as Morris Chestnut, with the same dazzling smile and skin the color of dark chocolate. She burst into tears, thankful to see someone who could help her.

The detective rapped his fist against the table. "This isn't over," he sneered as he rose and left the room.

The attorney sat and smiled, extending a hand to Karisma. "I'm Attorney Benjamin Hightower. I'm here to help you."

Karisma attempted to respond, but instead of words, vomit rose to the base of her throat. She turned her face, and it catapulted from her mouth, landing on the floor beside her chair. The stench alone made her hurl again.

She continued to hold her head down as her attorney jumped up and knocked on the door, signaling for the officer standing in the hallway.

Upon opening the door, the officer's eyes immediately traveled to the foul-smelling puke that covered a considerable portion of the floor beside her chair. He looked at her attorney and said nonchalantly, "I'll bring you a mop."

Attorney Hightower shook his head and argued, "I'm not cleaning that up...you are."

The officer smirked callously. "That's not my job. I can call janitorial services, but I can't guarantee when they'll get here. So, which do you prefer?"

"Fine. Bring me the mop," Attorney Hightower answered between clenched teeth. "Also bring my client something to settle her stomach," he ordered as the officer was closing the door behind himself.

The door ajar, he answered, "I'll bring her a cup of water." Her attorney stood next to the door and waited.

Karisma felt less nauseous but still horrible. She wiped her mouth with the sleeve of her sweatshirt and returned her head to the table.

She hadn't felt this humiliated since high school. Thoughts of cutting herself began to resurface, but she tried her best to cast them down.

After the officer returned with the mop and water, her attorney cleaned the floor. Then he sat opposite her. "I'm sorry we didn't meet under better circumstances," he said softly. "If it's any consolation, I'm going to get you out of here as soon as possible."

"How soon will that be?" She lifted her head, temples throbbing. With shaky hands, she picked up the small paper cup and sipped the water.

"I wish I could say *immediately*, but they're likely charging you with murder. So, unfortunately, there's no way around you appearing before a judge first. But I promise I'll do everything I can to get you on tomorrow's docket." His tone was light and hopeful.

"And if you can?" she asked exuberantly.

He sighed, placed his pen on the table, and leaned forward. With clasped hands, he answered, "I'm not going to sugarcoat things. Getting bond will be difficult." Dejected, Karisma crossed her arms and clenched her teeth, trying to push back thoughts of cutting herself.

"*But*," he continued. "It's my understanding you come from a good home, have never been in trouble, and you're not a flight risk... so hopefully we can get you out in the next day or so."

"Are my parents here?"

He shook his head. "I haven't spoken with your parents yet."

Confused, she furrowed her brow. "So how did you know I was here?"

"Your boss, LaShaun Delaney, retained me."

"Ohhh." Karisma didn't know whether to be thankful or worried. "Can you call my parents and tell them where I am, please?"

"Sure. I'll get the contact information before I leave. I know you're not feeling well, but we need to talk. Okay?"

"Yes, but can I lay my head on this table?"

"Anything to make it comfortable for you." He took a legal pad and pen from his black leather satchel and placed them on the table. "Now, did the officers say anything about the evidence they have against you?"

"Yes. They said they found Mr. Thomas's checkbook and license in my footlocker, and his jacket on the floor of my closet. Somebody must be trying to frame me."

She lifted her head to watch as he wrote down her response. The small pen seemed to be lost in his big hand. Only the tip was visible when he wrote.

"I believe I know the answer, but I must ask. Have you ever met Mr. Thomas, been in his presence...seen him at the church?"

"No sir. He was already dead when I started working at the church."

He nodded. "Good. Do you have any idea how his items could've ended up in your dorm room?"

Karisma sighed and shook her head. "I've been trying to figure that out. I promise you...I've never seen those items." She wrung her hands.

"What about your roommate? Could she have planted them there?" He studied her closely.

Karisma answered quickly. "I don't think so. We've gotten close since school began. She'd have no reason to do something like that."

He put his pen down and spoke sternly. "Someone who has access to your room had to have planted those items there. How can you be sure it wasn't your roommate?"

Karisma tried to think of a reason why she would do something like that, but she couldn't. She also couldn't say for certain that she wouldn't.

"I guess I can't be," she answered hesitantly. "I just don't know what motive she would have to do that."

He wrote *Investigate Roommate* in big bold letters. Then, he wrote *Get Insurance and Police Report* as he said, "Delaney already told me about the car. Has it been located?"

"No. You can get the insurance reports from my mom."

He smiled. "I will." She fidgeted in her seat.

He waited for her to stop moving. When she stopped and looked at him, he spoke.

"I don't have any further questions, but I want to talk to you about the process."

"Okay." She paid close attention.

"The state's attorney is called the District Attorney. He has the burden to prove you committed the crime you are accused of...do you understand that."

"Yes, Sir."

"I have the job of planting doubt in the mind of the judge, jury, and the public." Karisma gave him a puzzled look, so he explained further.

"The judge isn't going to be trying this case, but he'll be making some evidentiary rulings. He'll more likely rule in our favor if there's doubt in his mind about your guilt."

"I get it," Karisma responded.

"Your case is getting a lot of publicity, so we have to win the social media trial before we can get a victory in the courtroom. Our jurors will be privy to all types of opinions from social media and television pundits, and they will try to convict you before the judge bangs his gavel."

Before the attorney could continue, an officer slid back into the room. "Time to end this little get-together," he said. Attorney Hightower acknowledged with a nod.

"Here, jot down your parents' contact information." He slid his legal pad over to Karisma with an ink pen. As she finished writing, another officer entered the room.

"Stand up inmate." He barked.

She looked at her attorney, and he nodded. She stood slowly.

"Turn around," the officer directed. When she complied, he cuffed her.

"Don't worry...I got you," Attorney Hightower assured her before she was escorted from the room. "Don't talk to anyone about the case."

She shuttered when she heard the metal door clang behind her.

Chapter Fourteen
ALL MANNER OF LIES

Heiress stood in the doorway of her small *en suite* bathroom, brushing her teeth while watching the evening news on her bedroom television. Her expensive gold comforter was tossed to the floor like an unwanted dishrag, and Vic's nude body was stretched across the bed, waiting for round two.

Her hand came to a screeching halt as she watched a video of a police officer shoving someone in the backseat of his vehicle. *Karisma Stanley Arrested for the Murder of Archibald Thomas* was displayed at the bottom of the screen. Heiress rushed over to the dresser and stared at the television, blocking Vic's view.

Karisma's hands were cuffed behind her back, and an army of reporters swarmed the vehicle, asking why she killed Mr. Thomas, and whether she worked as an escort for Sweet Dreams Boutique.

Heiress gaped at the screen as minty toothpaste dripped from her open mouth.

"You know her?" Vic asked after the anchorman switched topics. Without answering, Heiress dashed to the bathroom to rinse her mouth and cleanse the toothpaste remnants from her face.

"What did you say?" she asked when she returned. She lifted the comforter from the floor.

"Do you know her...the girl they arrested?"

She threw the comforter on the bed and straightened it. Although she and Vic were growing closer, he was still a detective, so Heiress didn't want to reveal too much.

"Kinda," she answered nonchalantly. She was still dumbfounded by what she'd seen and prayed silently for Karisma's strength and well-being.

"I'm just asking because she's in a lot of trouble," he said matter-of-factly.

"Seems so," Heiress spat curtly. Vic tended to mansplain as if she were a child, and it agitated her. Sure, he was fifteen years older than her but, unlike many twenty-three-year-olds, she was very mature for her age and knowledgeable about the law. She'd worked at her mom's law office since middle school and had gone to court with her often.

She got in bed and tightened the comforter around her body, mind racing back to past encounters with Karisma: the women's conference, the sorority's meet-and-greet, and DMI. As much as Karisma was a mystery to Heiress, she didn't seem capable of murder.

"Are you okay?" Vic asked. "You look troubled."

"I think I'm a little shocked," Heiress conceded. "I have a hard time believing Karisma is capable of the horrible things they're accusing her of. Prostitution? Murder? I'm not buying it. She's way too intelligent to get caught up like that."

Vic shrugged. "You never know. Sex for pay on college campuses is common these days." He turned his body towards Heiress and placed his hand between her thighs. "All young girls have to do is find somebody willing to finance their education and lavish lifestyles in exchange for unlimited access to do what they want to their bodies." He began to rub between her legs.

Heiress tsked and moved his hands. "I'm sure nothing like that goes on at AU because no one's living a lavish lifestyle. If it weren't for the meal plan, many students would starve."

Vic sat up and swung his feet off the side of the bed. "The guys maybe. But where do you think the girls get the money to have their hair done, nails done... dress like baller wives?" he challenged.

"You look at too much television." She shook her head and picked up the remote to channel surf.

Vic laughed. "You know I'm right. Their moms and dads aren't paying for *everything* they're flexing on social media. And girls these days are easily lured into sex rings. The sad thing is...once they get in, sometimes the only way out is for them to kill."

Heiress shook her head. "*As a Work of Art*, I'm privy to all the scandalous tea. So, if something were going on at AU, I'd know about it."

"I hate to break it to you, but it has been going on for years."

Heiress looked at him suspiciously. "If that's true, why hasn't anyone been arrested?"

Vic went into the bathroom. "Karisma's the first."

The next morning, Heiress drove to DMI to speak with LaShaun. As much as she dreaded confronting her, she needed answers. If the rumors were true, she was determined to find out.

She pulled onto DMI's parking lot, just as LaShaun parked her car, hopped out, and darted towards the building. "Lady Delaney!" she hollered as she jumped out of her car and raced towards LaShaun. She was relieved when LaShaun stopped and waited for her to catch up.

"You are a sight for sore eyes, young lady." LaShaun pulled Heiress into a loving embrace. "Why didn't you let me know you were coming?"

"I didn't know I was dropping by until late last night. I was looking at the news, and I became worried about you. I mean, Karisma being accused of killing Deacon Thomas? It's got to be hard on you."

LaShaun didn't answer right away. She looked towards the sky and blinked rapidly. Then she grabbed a tissue from her purse and dabbed the corners of her eyes.

"I still can't believe it. Couldn't sleep at all last night." She glumly straightened the hem of her black suit jacket.

"Are you sure you need to be working? Let me take you home." Heiress brushed a hand across LaShaun's shoulder.

LaShaun pulled her long sleek ponytail. "I'm good," she sighed. "Just stopped by to pick something up before I head to Karisma's bond hearing."

Heiress's eyes bulged, and she put her right hand to her mouth. "It's today? It hasn't even been 24 hours since her arrest."

LaShaun shrugged. "I guess she has a good lawyer." For obvious reasons, she wanted to keep news of her involvement a secret. Neither Deacon Thomas's family nor the church congregation would take kindly to her aiding the person accused of his murder.

Heiress saw LaShaun's visit to the courthouse as an opportunity to be there for both ladies while hearing the evidence against

Karisma at the same time. That way she could gauge the truth for herself. "Do you mind if I ride with you?"

"You know you don't have to ask. I'd love the company." The cloud lifted from LaShaun's face. "Go on to my car while I pick up what I need from Langston."

Neither Heiress nor LaShaun said much on the ride over to the courthouse. The uncertainty in the air was thick. Twenty minutes after arriving and passing through security, the ladies walked into Courtroom 3B.

Beyond the bar, attorneys and court personnel milled about. In the gallery, spectators looked at their phones or whispered to each other as they awaited the judge's arrival. Heiress and LaShaun looked for a place to sit in the crowded courtroom.

Heiress followed behind LaShaun as a DMI member waved them over to the third bench. She noticed the woman's smile fade into a frown when she had to make room for two bodies instead of one. Heiress knew her from the usher's ministry and wanted to check her for her sour attitude, but the bailiff called the court to order.

"Be seated," Judge Peale ordered as he took his seat and scanned the courtroom. Wasting no time, he gave orders for how spectators were to govern themselves, then called the case of State v. Stanley. "DA Muhammad, is the prosecution ready?"

A brown-skinned woman in her early forties, with long braids forming a knot at the nape of her neck, a long slender nose, and almond-shaped eyes stood and announced, "Yes, Your Honor."

He looked at Attorney Hightower and asked him the same question, to which he responded, "Ready, Your Honor."

Judge Peale looked at the bailiff and nodded. "Bring in the Defendant."

Heiress heard a controlled whimper and looked over to see a

middle-aged woman lean on a man who sat stoically beside her as Karisma entered the room from a side door.

Her orange jumpsuit was made for someone three times her size, and her thick white socks kept her black shower shoes from properly fitting her feet. The chain that connected her handcuffs to the cuffs encircling both ankles made it difficult for her to walk with a normal gait. All eyes were on her as she slowly shuffled from the door to the defendant's table.

The beautiful weave she normally sported had been replaced with two braids, each resting along the sides of her head. Gone was the vibrant made-up doll Heiress was used to seeing. Looking at her, you couldn't tell whether she was educated or uneducated, wealthy, or poor.

After she stood at her seat, Judge Peale read the charges against her, and she pleaded, "Not Guilty." He then moved to the bond hearing, where her attorney asked the court to set a reasonable bond. The judge then looked to the prosecutor. "What's the State's position?" he asked authoritatively.

Prosecutor Muhammad peered at the paper she held, folded it, and placed it on the table.

"Your honor, the State opposes. The defendant is a member of an elaborate sex ring that has been operating on the campus of Atlanta University for many years. When Mr. Archibald Thomas lost consciousness in the Lancaster Hotel on December nineteenth, the defendant fled the scene and left him for dead.

On December 27th, when it appeared he would recover, she entered his hospital room and disconnected his pacemaker, causing him to suffer another heart attack."

Without warning, Kari stood and shouted, "You murderer!" Spectators gasped in shock as she aimed her finger in Karisma's direction, pronouncing, "You're gonna rot in he-."

Kairo immediately placed his hands over Kari's mouth and begged her to take a seat and calm down. The judge rapidly banged his gavel as he tried to regain control of his courtroom. Kari refused to be silenced and attempted to pull Kairo's hands from her mouth.

She somehow tore from his grasp and lunged in Karisma's direction. Trampling people to get to the other side of the courtroom, she screeched, "You better hope you stay behind bars, B-.' Kairo grabbed her with his left arm and covered her mouth as additional officers barged through the door.

The judge banged his gavel quicker and with greater force. Angrily and repetitively, he shouted, "Order in my court! Order in my court!" When everyone calmed down, he looked at Kari and growled, "Officers, remove her from the courtroom before I am forced to find her in contempt!"

All eyes followed the riveting spectacle, except Kairo. He held his forehead in his hands and shook his head in disbelief. When the door closed behind Kari and the officers, the judge continued.

"If I hear *anyone* make a sound other than the DA and defense attorney, I will hold them in contempt and remove everyone from this courtroom for the duration of these proceedings. Am I *clear?*"

Seething, he took off his eyeglasses and scanned the courtroom, daring anyone to say a word. When he was satisfied, he barked, "DA Muhammad, you may continue." She promptly obeyed.

"Your honor, due to the heinous nature of this crime, the defendant having no familial ties to the community, and her danger to others, the State opposes bail and asks that she remain in custody pending trial."

Judge Peale turned to Attorney Hightower, who jumped from his seat.

"Your honor, Karisma Stanley is joined here today by her

parents, Deyja and Quinton Stanton, both upstanding citizens who were born and raised here in Atlanta. They attended Spelman and Morehouse, respectively. Karisma Stanley is a junior at Atlanta University and has a 3.5-grade point average. She desires to continue her education, Your Honor. And I repeat, the charges against her are circumstantial.

She has never been in trouble with the law and is not a flight risk or a danger to the community. Justice is not served by continuing to have her incarcerated pending trial. Even if she can't remain in school pending trial, she can be monitored by the probation office in Savannah."

The prosecutor tried her best to negate his argument, but Attorney Hightower prevailed. Judge Peale set bail at one million dollars and ordered Karisma to wear an ankle monitor.

After bail was announced, Heiress turned to LaShaun, incredulous. "In what world is that reasonable? How can she afford that?"

Leaning over, LaShaun whispered casually, "A bondsman will post the million dollars, and Karisma's family will only pay him ten percent of that."

Heiress sat stunned; one hundred thousand is still a lot of money for a family to pay in one lump sum. To LaShaun who had everything, it seemed like it was no big deal; to Heiress, it would take a lot to garner that much money.

As Karisma was led out of the courtroom, she glanced at her mom. The weariness in her eyes was so gut-wrenching, that Karisma doubled over and cried out sorrowfully, "I didn't do it, Mom. I promise I didn't do it."

Chapter Fifteen

NEAR THE CROSS

LaShaun and Heiress sprinted into the hallway as Kari ranted about the injustice of allowing the person who killed her father back on the streets. She ran up to LaShaun and pushed her as she yelled, "You knew she was a killer and you said nothing! You are just as guilty as she is. You should be behind bars too!"

An older gentleman grabbed Kari by the waist, pulling her backward. He clamped his beefy hand over her mouth, muffling the tirade of curses she spewed out.

"I'm so sorry First Lady," he mouthed. LaShaun mouthed "It's fine," in return, and raced in the opposite direction, towards the stairwell. Miraculously, Heiress was the only one who followed while the gaggle of reporters busied themselves trying to interview Kari.

As the door slammed behind them, LaShaun gripped the railing as she regained her composure. After a few minutes passed, she smoothed her hair and a hand over her clothes, then moved to go back inside. Heiress grabbed her by the arm, stopping her. "Are you sure you want to go back in there?" she asked.

"Sure. Kari's upset. I get it. Her father was murdered, and the prime suspect was just granted bail. She's reacting out of pain, and I understand that very well." She didn't like being the object of Kari's angst, but she wasn't going to cower and hide out in a stairwell.

"Still, let's wait a little longer." Heiress pleaded. "Kari's ready to beat the crap out of somebody." She rested a hand on LaShaun's shoulder. "Give her time to calm down."

"Don't worry, her bark is bigger than her bite." She took Heiress's hand in hers and squeezed it before opening the door and heading back inside.

The hallway was bustling with activity as lawyers reviewed plea deals, case strategies, and direct examinations with their clients. Kari, Kairo, and the media were gone. LaShaun asked Heiress to leave and bring the car around to the front of the courthouse while she talked to a friend.

Heiress wondered who she would be talking to, but she dared not ask. Instead, she looked around as she walked down the hall to see if anyone looked familiar.

LaShaun scanned the crowd until she spotted Attorney Hightower. As she strutted towards him, a tall, slender, well-dressed woman who appeared to be in her early fifties approached him. She recognized her from the courtroom; Karisma's mother.

LaShaun paused where she was and stood against the wall - close enough to hear their conversation. She allowed them to talk about bail logistics, then walked over to introduce herself as Attorney Hightower pulled paperwork from his satchel.

LaShaun hugged Attorney Hightower, and he introduced her

to Deyja. LaShaun greeted her with a warm handshake, and Deyja reluctantly shook it.

Despite her hesitancy, LaShaun spoke. "Mrs. Stanley, I want to tell you what a wonderful daughter you have. She-"

"I already know what kind of daughter I have. What I don't know is how she got mixed up with someone like you," Deyja snapped.

LaShaun was unprepared for Deyja's brash response. She rarely encountered anyone with the gall to address her in such a forthright manner. Usually, people talked about her behind her back. This woman was brazen enough to challenge her to her face.

Lashaun cocked her neck. "First, watch that tone! I'm not the one and this ain't the day!"

Attorney Hightower was mortified. He immediately placed his body between them. "Please excuse Mrs. Stanley, the arrest has taken a toll on her. She doesn't mean to be so rude." He peered at Deyja with disdain.

"Don't speak for me!" Deyja snapped. She darted an index finger at LaShaun. "Have you been pimping out my daughter?"

Attorney Hightower started to speak, but LaShaun held up her hand and stopped him. She knew pain when she saw it, and she was very sorry for the uphill battle Karisma and her family now face.

With all the civility she could muster, LaShaun said, "I assure you that I've done nothing but hire your daughter at DMI so she could earn money to help pay tuition. Everything you heard in the courtroom is a bunch of lies curated by an overzealous prosecutor. Karisma is an outstanding young lady, and I have no doubt she has been wrongfully accused."

Deyja stared at LaShaun in silence for a moment. "Well, I don't know what to believe, so I'm going to roll with that for now. But if

I find out anything different, these size tens will be in your behind, I can promise you that!"

LaShaun looked to her right and then her left. "Look heifer, you ain't the only one with shoes. And I guarantee you my legs are longer, and my foot is bigger. Now jump if you want to!"

Attorney Hightower held LaShaun's arms and addressed Deyja.

"Look Lady, you have LaShaun Delaney to thank for hiring me *and* getting Karisma on the docket so fast. If it weren't for her, you wouldn't be able to take your daughter home today. So, I suggest you show her a little more respect."

Deyja glared at LaShaun defiantly. LaShaun returned her stare with greater venom. Realizing LaShaun wasn't backing down, Deyja thanked her, halfheartedly.

LaShaun replied, "You're welcome." She respected Deyja's willingness to go hard for her child. If her child was in a similar predicament, she knew she'd go even harder. But one thing she wasn't going to do is allow Deyja to punk her.

"If Karisma needs anything at all, please don't hesitate to ask," LaShaun added.

Deyja looked at LaShaun with a perplexed frown. "Why are you so interested in helping my daughter? According to the news, Mr. Thomas was a deacon at your church."

LaShaun sniffed. "Yes, he was. And I want to find his killer as much as anyone, but I don't think it's Karisma. I believe the killer is still running around free, and I'll do everything in my power to help your daughter beat the charges so the police will be *forced* to find the real perpetrator."

"Of course," Deyja responded, warily. "That's mighty kind of you, but Karisma's father and I can take care of her just fine. That's our job." She forced a tight smile.

LaShaun looked around. "And where is your husband? I want to introduce myself."

Attorney Hightower responded quickly. "He had a few calls to make to secure bail. We'd better be leaving. We'll catch up later." He pleaded with his eyes for LaShaun to leave.

"Alright. Well, I wish you all the best Mrs. Stanley. Please tell Karisma her job is waiting when she gets out."

"Oh, my daughter won't be coming back," Deyja hissed. "The dean of students called me this morning. Karisma's been expelled from school. She's coming home."

LaShaun smiled and responded snidely, "I can help you with that, too. I sit on the board."

Deyja turned her back to LaShaun. "We're good. As I said, my daughter's coming home."

LaShaun briefly closed her eyes and prayed silently. *Jesus, keep me near the cross.* Then she turned and addressed Attorney Hightower.

"Send me your bill from this morning, please. Mrs. Stanley said she can take it from here." She spun on her heels and strolled to the elevator with her head held high.

Deyja stared at Attorney Hightower with a look of surprise on her face. "I thought you were court appointed. How much will it cost me to retain your services?"

He didn't have the heart to tell her his astronomical fee. He charged top dollar because he was the top dog in the legal arena. "Just focus on getting Karisma released, and we'll cross the next bridge when we come to it," he answered.

"Ok. Well, thanks for what you did today. I really appreciate it."

"Don't thank me, thank LaShaun Delaney. I wouldn't be here if it weren't for her. She is probably your only hope if you want Karisma cleared of these charges."

Deyja didn't want anything to do with LaShaun Delaney. She stayed as far away from religious folk as she possibly could. They were all sinful, judgmental hypocrites as far as she was concerned.

She'd seen the worst of church folk and wanted no parts of anyone's religion. She warned Karisma not to work at DMI, but her warnings were ignored. Now looked where she was.

"I will have my husband call you when we get Karisma home. You can talk over your fee with him," she said as she extended her hand to shake his.

"Certainly. I'll await his call." He re-entered the courtroom as Deyja headed towards the elevator. When she finally made it out front, the camera crew and LaShaun Delaney were nowhere to be found.

Thirty minutes later, Heiress pushed the button to open the garage to LaShaun's home and eased in. LaShaun had fallen asleep, and Heiress didn't want to awaken her. She stared at the beautifully made-up face and wondered if the rumors were true.

For the past few years, Heiress had been closer to LaShaun than her own mother, and she had a hard time believing anything but the best about her. But she didn't want to be naïve.

"What's on your mind, Heiress?" LaShaun's eyes remained closed.

"Nothing. I didn't want to wake you. You seem so tired."

"Are you sure that's it or are you wondering if the news reports are true?"

Heiress was afraid to show that she doubted LaShaun, but she needed answers. She would never turn her back on her, but she also didn't want to end up in jail like Karisma. The truth would give her what she needed to decide whether to continue her relationship with Vic or not. She wouldn't remain with him if LaShaun were the real target of his investigation.

"I guess I'm wondering if the reports are true," she answered sheepishly.

LaShaun opened her eyes and turned her torso towards Heiress. She never wanted her involved in the inner workings of Sweet Dreams Boutique, and her position remained.

She'd done everything she could to help Heiress have a good life, free of drama and free of the issues that were born from having too much knowledge. No, she would not tell Heiress anything.

"The news reporters have it wrong. They are in the business of making money, and they don't care whom they hurt. I do not run a sex trafficking ring. Sweet Dreams Boutique is a legitimate and prosperous business. Some don't like that. They want to take Langston and me down, and they will use all manner of lies to do it."

Heiress wanted desperately to believe her, so she did. She decided she would accept her answer and wouldn't question her anymore. She'd worked with LaShaun for several years and knew people were out to get them. Their success begat enemies and backbiters. Unfortunately, it went with the territory.

Chapter Sixteen
HOLD ON TO HOPE

The past 24 hours had been miserable. While birds chirped and bees buzzed, welcoming the arrival of Spring, Karisma had been in a cold, disgusting, holding cell wondering what the future held for her.

She was mentally and physically exhausted. Spending the night on a cold steel bench- surrounded by drunks, prostitutes, and drug mules-pushed her to her breaking point.

First, there was *Baby Girl*, who was darker than night and donned a long blond weave that bobbed from left to right as she performed strip tease against the bars of the cell. Then there was *Rabbit*, who was either drunk or high out of her mind and spent the entire night hopping from one cellmate to another asking, "You got a hit?"

Traumatized, Karisma kept her eyes glued to the filthy floor as she rocked back and forth, chanting "Mind over matter," repeatedly.

She was close to dozing off when she heard one of the guards call out, "Stanley!"

She jerked her head towards the cell door and was greeted by a former linebacker turned guard. Fear seized her as she struggled to answer. "Get up!" he commanded when nothing came out.

She hurried to the steel bars as her cellmates demanded he takes them too.

"Turn around and put your hands behind your back."

She quickly obeyed. "Where are you taking me?"

"You're going before the judge," he said aggressively. Her cellmates insisted they were scheduled to see the judge also. He ignored them as he opened the cell door and retrieved Karisma.

She sat in another area of the detention center for an hour as other inmates were gathered from different parts of the facility. At one-thirty, they were transported to the courthouse.

Her mother always swore she would never visit a child of hers in jail. Karisma was grateful her threat didn't extend to the courthouse. Because sitting in the first row of the hearing room were her parents. *Thank God I don't have to go through this alone.*

Her relief didn't last long, for she could see disappointment etched on their faces.

She'd grown up hearing how her parents had spent thousands, enrolling her in the finest schools and admitting her to the most prominent social groups. Deyja made sure her daughter was exposed to debutante balls, the ballet, and any other upper echelon societal event there was. She consistently admonished Karisma not to forget all the things her love for her provided. The one thing Deyja neglected to do, was tell Karisma, "I love you."

Now, she was forced to sit silently as the district attorney painted the picture of a young woman who was so addicted to money and frills, that she was willing to sell her body and kill anyone who threatened the lifestyle she'd grown accustomed to. She cringed in her seat and dug her thumbnail into the palm of her hand as she stared into Judge Peale's eyes.

She straightened her back and rubbed her stinging hands when Attorney Hightower pointed out that she had strong familial support, stellar academics, and no criminal record. Thankfully, Judge Peale accepted his argument and granted bail, despite the outcry from the deacon's daughter.

She thought she'd go home with her parents immediately. However, she had to return to jail to be processed out. Again, she waited. Again, she worried.

At six o'clock that evening, she was released into her father's custody. He looked worn and haggard despite the navy, tailored suit, and red polka-dot tie he wore.

While walking out of the building, Karisma took in his tall, slender frame, and noticed his hair was graying around the edges. His skin, the color of caramel and just as smooth, didn't hide the tiny lines starting to assemble along the outside corner of his eyes.

"Where's Mom?" she asked as her father took the plastic bag containing her belongings from her.

"She's been through a lot today. She stayed home to rest," he said wearily.

She's been through a lot? What about me? Karisma sighed with her head held down. Her father pulled her to him and kissed the crown of her head. It went a long way toward melting the hardness forming in her heart. She needed to know and feel she was still worthy of her parent's love.

On the ride home, she felt her father needed to hear she was innocent. He needed to know all he'd poured into her was not in vain.

"I'm being set up, Dad! I promise I haven't done the terrible things I'm being accused of. You raised me right. Rod can clear this up - he was the one driving my car that night. He got me into this mess!"

Mr. Stanley looked at her briefly, then slammed his fists against the steering wheel. Small bits of spittle flew out of his mouth as he yelled. "What have I told you about lending out your car? Especially to your no-good cousin. You know what kind of lifestyle Rod leads. Why don't you listen when I tell you something?"

Karisma didn't answer him. She couldn't. Because he was correct. Rod had always been classified as a juvenile delinquent. He'd been in and out of trouble since middle school-selling pills, stealing cars, and fighting. But Karisma loved him like a brother. They'd grown up together. And, when she was with Rod, she'd always felt safe... always felt seen.

She bolted from the car and raced inside the house as soon as Quinton parked the car. Bypassing her parents' room, she dashed into her room, slamming the door behind her. She hurried to the bathroom and turned the shower on its hottest setting, then gathered her pajama set, shampoo, and conditioner, taking them inside the bathroom with her.

There was no way to wash away the memory of the past twenty-four hours, but at least she could scrub the prison residue off her skin. She stayed in the shower for an hour, washing from head to toe. When she finished, she turned on the rain shower and let the water wash over her body as she tried to forget the trauma she'd experienced. When she got to bed, her exhaustion lulled her to sleep.

The next morning the smell of a home-cooked meal awakened her. It had been a day since she'd eaten, and her stomach growled from the lack of food. She wanted to remain in bed, but her rumbling stomach compelled her to get up and get dressed. She was near the kitchen when the sound of Deyja speaking to her sister -Karisma's Aunt Tracey, stopped her in the hallway.

"I told you I haven't heard from that boy," Tracey insisted in a firm voice.

"Well, we need to find him, Tracey! My baby's in serious trouble because of Rod. Have you contacted the police?" The sound of bacon sizzling and utensils clanging against pots didn't drown out the anxiousness in Deyja's quivering voice.

Oh, so you do care, Karisma thought.

"Girl, you know I don't get the police involved in my life," Tracey retorted.

"That's fine for you, but because of your son, I've got the police involved in mine. I need you to find Rod so he can straighten out this mess! Where does he normally hang out?"

"I don't know."

"Girl, you do know. Don't play me!" Deyja pointed at her with the wooden spatula.

Normally, she made sure to always speak in a manner that conveyed her current socio-economic status. When she graduated from college and become an accountant, she left the 'hood talk' back in the projects where she'd grown up. But when she's angry...sophistication goes out the window.

As soon as Karisma stepped into the kitchen, Tracey jumped up and wrapped her in a long warm embrace.

"Hey, sweetheart. I'm so sorry you're having to go through this. How are you holding up?"

Terrified. Lonely. Depressed. "I'm fine," Karisma lied. She looked over at Deyja; she was hovering over the stove stirring grits.

Karisma and Tracey sat at the table across from each other,

and Tracey gently took Karisma's hand in hers. "You don't have to be brave for any of us, baby. I know this isn't easy, but you'll get through this. And I'm gonna find Rod so he can help you clear all this up, okay?"

"If you wanted to find Rod, you would've done so already," Deyja snapped. She waved the wooden spoon in the air. "Don't feed my child those lies! Giving her false hope."

Tracey rolled her eyes and turned back to her niece. "Karisma baby, hold onto hope. You have God on your side, and He will get you through this. My whole church is praying for you, and the prayers of the righteous availeth much."

"Mmm hmmm," Deyja taunted with a twisted laugh.

Tracy looked at Deyja disdainfully. "Pay your mama no mind. She's been lost a long time. Maybe this is the one thing that can bring her back to Christ. I'm praying it will. As my pastor says, 'Hell is too hot, judgment is too dreadful, and eternity is *too long* for y'all to mess around and miss Heaven.'"

"Don't start your foolishness today, Tracey. I am not in the mood!" Deyja warned.

"I'm not starting anything," Tracey defended. "I'm here to console my niece. And there is no better consolation than that offered by the Lord Jesus Christ." She held up her hands in praise. "You knew that before you became so uppity."

Every time they're in each other's company, Deyja and Tracey argue. And neither is willing to back down or apologize. That's the way the sisters handle things, and Karisma stays out of it. Because once the argument runs its course, they move on like nothing ever happened.

"Hand me your plate, Kay."

"Yes Ma'am," Karisma responded as she stood and went to the cabinet.

"What did her attorney say?" Tracey asked calmly.

Deyja did not look at Tracey, but she answered, "He's not her attorney. He's someone LaShaun Delaney hired to represent Kay at the hearing."

Tracey clutched her imaginary pearls. "*The* LaShaun Delaney? How in the world do you know *her*?"

"I don't know her," Deyja clarified. "Karisma met her at a women's conference and worked for her."

Tracey playfully swatted the air. "That's big-time baby girl. Why haven't you mentioned that before now?"

"I never thought it was important," Karisma responded. She spread strawberry preserves on her toast with a butter knife.

"My daughter is not impressed by *no* LaShaun Delaney," Deyja said coldly as she placed her plate on the table and sat down. "She's just another woman. Being the *first lady* doesn't make her no better than anyone else."

"Stop hating," Tracey scolded as she tore into her bacon. "That woman is a nationally known author, speaker, philanthropist, and Woman of God."

"You left out pimp," Deyja quipped.

"There you go. Any time a black person makes it in life, people try to tear 'em down. Like they can't run a prosperous business. You know how that feels, yet here you are, doing the same doggone thing." She drank her juice.

"I'm not tearing anyone down. I just know there's more to that sista than meets the eye. And because of LaShaun Delaney, my child is caught up in some mess that could cost her freedom." Her voice croaked the last words.

Karisma kept quiet as Tracey scooted her chair over and reached to pull Deyja into an embrace. Deyja held her hand out like a stop sign to keep her from getting too close. Tracey pushed it down and hugged her anyway.

"Look, Karisma's going to be alright, okay? Don't you ever forget that. You may not have faith, but I have enough for us all. God will never leave her or forsake her."

Deyja didn't know if that were true, but she had no strength to dispute it. Karisma took in her aunt's words and wondered, *Is this the thing God is using to bring me back to Him?*

Chapter Seventeen
THE STORM IS COMING

Later that day, while visiting Savannah with her mom, Heiress had a strong urge to visit Karisma. She'd been praying for her but figured she needed to see a familiar face, someone who didn't believe the lies that were spreading on social media.

Her gray stucco home sat at the top of a hill. Purple Hydrangea and Pink Rose bushes lined the front and sides of the home, making it warm and inviting. As she walked up the long driveway, she convinced herself surprising Karisma was the right decision. When Deyja answered the door with a scowl on her face, she immediately reconsidered.

"Yes, can I help you?" Deyja snapped.

"Umm, my name is Heiress Storm, and I was hoping I could speak to Karisma," she stammered.

"What do you want with Karisma?" Deyja asked harshly.

Heiress licked her lips. "I know her from AU, and just wanted to offer her some support since she's going through such a tough time."

Deyja looked Heiress up and down like she was trying to decide which limb to rip from her body first. Heiress smiled uneasily as Deyja sized her up.

"Karisma, you've got company," Deyja yelped as she stepped aside and held the door open for Heiress to enter.

Heiress tried not to gawk when she walked over the threshold into the foyer but couldn't help herself. The spectacular furnishing and decor could rival that found in any home and garden magazine.

Karisma was halfway down the stairs when she saw Karisma and stopped. "Hey, what are you doing here?" she asked warily.

Heiress looked up at her. "I wanted to make sure you're okay. I can't imagine what you must be going through, but I figured a friendly face might help."

"That was nice of you. Thanks," Karisma responded skeptically.

Deyja stood off to the side like a pit bull as Karisma walked down the stairs, then directed Heiress to the living room.

"Are you from around here, Heiress?" Deyja asked. She sat at the edge of the sofa.

"No ma'am. My mom and I are visiting a relative. I'm from Alpharetta, near Atlanta."

"I'm familiar. Who are your parents?"

Unnerved, Heiress reminded herself not to fidget and tried hard to keep her voice from shaking. "Hamilton and Johnysa Storm."

"I don't think I know them. What kind of work do they do?"

"My father works for Homeland Security, and my mother's an attorney." Heiress didn't think it prudent to tell her Hamilton left them for another woman, and Johnysa is depressed and unemployed.

"Hmph," Deyja replied. She gave Heiress a good once-over and left the girls alone.

I'm sorry, Karisma mouthed as her mother disappeared. Her braids were piled into a bun on top of her head, and small diamond studs were in her ears. Faint freckles dotted her skin, and she looked much better than when Heiress had last seen her. However, her gold joggers and white cropped t-shirt highlighted her significant weight loss.

"I didn't know your mother's an attorney," Karisma said when they were alone.

"One of the best criminal defense attorneys in Atlanta," Heiress boasted proudly. "She was a fixer before *Olivia Pope* knew anything needed fixing. Your attorney is supposedly one of the best also."

Karisma lowered her voice and leaned close to Heiress. "He's not my attorney any longer. I overheard my parents say he was hired by Lady Delaney, and my mother's adamant about hiring someone else to handle the case since she wants nothing to do with her."

"Why?" Heiress whispered. "She has a lot of connections, and it could only help you to have her in your corner."

"Not if she's pimping out girls and setting me up for murder," Karisma said matter-of-factly.

"What? You know that's not true!" Heiress said louder. "She would never do anything that foul."

Karisma scoffed. "So, you really think it's lingerie she's selling for thousands of dollars?"

"Definitely. If a purse can cost fifteen thousand, why can't lingerie sell for thousands? You think Oprah would raise an eyebrow at that amount?"

"Everybody ain't Oprah," Karisma countered.

"True, but everybody ain't broke either. We're judging Sweet

Dream's prices because we can't afford them. We can't fathom paying that amount because we don't have the money. If we did, we wouldn't be having this conversation."

"I hope that's true. But the DA is convinced otherwise and is determined to prove it."

Deyja entered the room and notified them it was time for lunch. Karisma stood up first.

"Thanks, but I better be leaving, I didn't mean to intrude." Heiress rose from the sofa.

Deyja smiled pleasantly. "Nonsense. You're welcome to stay. There's plenty."

"Please stay," Karisma begged. "You're the first visitor I've had." She grabbed Heiress's hand and pulled her into the kitchen with her.

A banquette that seats five was in front of a large rectangular window, and a round table was in the middle, flanked by three white leather chairs. The tabletop was white marble with gray swirls and matched the kitchen island. A round silver serving tray was in the center, with tea sandwiches, nuts, fruit, and petit fours.

When they sat down, Deyja handed them both a warm damp towel to wipe their hands. She held a small tray, and when they were finished, they placed the towels on it. Then, she left the room.

"My, my, my! Aren't we fancy!" Heiress kidded in a British accent. She placed her gray linen napkin across her lap and used tongs to grab her tea sandwiches.

Karisma giggled. Then, looking down her nose and mirroring Heiress's accent, she joked, "Welcome to the House of Ston-ley. Please enjoy your tea and crumpets."

They both roared with laughter. When they finished eating, they went to Karisma's room to watch television.

"Wow!" Heiress marveled as she entered the room. The bed was made, the books on the bookshelf were straight, the desk in the corner was dusted, no clothes or shoes were in view, and you could eat off the rug that covered the hardwood floor.

"Do you always keep your room this clean, or do you have a maid?"

"Neither. My mom does the cleaning. No one else can meet her outrageous standards." She plopped on her bed, and Heiress sat at her desk.

"I wish my mom would clean mine." Heiress looked at her watch and read the text message from her mom.

"No, you don't. It's not all it's cracked up to be. Trust me." Karisma turned on the television.

"I'm sorry, but my mom just texted me. She's ready to head back to Atlanta." Heiress got up to leave.

Karisma met her at the door to her room. "I was having such a great time. Take me with you," she pleaded playfully.

Heiress smiled. "I wish I could. Maybe next time, my friend." They walked down the hall together.

When they reached the front door, Heiress asked, "If your parents fired your attorney, who are they going to get to represent you?"

"I have no idea. I'm just happy to be home until my trial."

"I'm glad you are too. I don't wish jail on my worst enemies. If your parents can't find a good attorney, let me know. I can try to coax Mom into handling your case."

"I'll talk to them about it tonight. What's your mother's name again?"

"Johnysa Storm," Heiress announced with pride. She took one of her mom's business cards from her purse and scratched out the office number. She added her mom's cell phone number and handed it to Karisma. "Don't hesitate to call if you need her."

"Thanks," Karisma said. When they reached the door, she crossed her forearms and made a fist with her hands, simulating a *Black Panther* Wakanda farewell. "I'll let you know what my parents decide."

Later that night Heiress called Johnysa to give her a heads up about Karisma. Johnysa had spent several months in therapy and was doing well. She'd reopened her practice and seemed to be forging ahead stronger than ever.

"Mom, have you heard about the case regarding a deacon at DMI who was killed?"

"Of course, it's all over the news," Johnysa said. "LaShaun Delaney strikes again."

Heiress ignored the dig. Her mom always claimed LaShaun was the devil in disguise but never said why she believed it to be true.

"Well, that's why I'm call-"

"What does that case have to do with you?" Johnysa cut Heiress off before she had an opportunity to finish her sentence. "LaShaun better not have you nowhere near her mess!"

Heiress moved the phone from her ears and held it against her forehead, briefly. Then she returned it to her ear and responded slowly, "Listen for one minute, please. I'm friends with the girl who was arrested."

Johnysa raised her voice. "Why are you friends with someone who's going around selling her body?"

Heiress rolled her eyes. "She's not selling her body. Stop going by what you hear on television."

"With LaShaun in the mix, *anything* is possible."

Perturbed, Heiress asked, "Why do you hate her so much?"

Johnysa let out a deep sigh. "I don't hate her. I just know her better than you ever will. Ask your daddy. He knows her even better than I."

Heiress shook her head in frustration. "What's that supposed to mean?" She held up her hand. "You know what, don't answer that. My friend needs your help. She's not going to be acquitted unless she has a beast on her side, and that's you." She flashed a weak smile, hoping to soften up her mother.

"How do you even know she wants me to represent her?" Johnysa asked.

"I don't," Heiress chirped with a shrug. "She's going to talk to her parents about it- I'm just giving you a heads up."

"I'm letting you know now that if I do represent her, I'm coming after your precious LaShaun with both barrels if I need to."

"Calm down. There will be no need for all that. I worked for LaShaun for three years and..."

"...and you saw only what she allowed you to see. You think she would conduct that type of business openly?"

"I don't believe she would conduct that type of business at all." Heiress placed the phone on speaker and laid it on her dresser. She then opened the top drawer to pull out the tank and shorts she likes to sleep in.

"I know you don't, and that's okay. And I'll admit...she could have changed. For your sake, I hope she has. But I honestly can't put anything past her. We were best friends until she betrayed me."

Heiress could hear the sadness in her voice. "Mom, I'm so sorry. What happened?" Heiress anxiously awaited her response.

"Psst. That's water under the bridge now. I've made peace with it."

Heiress knew that wasn't true. Just the mention of LaShaun's name caused Johnysa to tense up and go into a tirade.

"Ok, Mom. I didn't mean to make you relive the past. I'll let you know if Karisma reaches out."

"And if she does, I'm warning you. The storm is coming."

They both laughed as they ended the call.

Chapter Eighteen
DELIVER ME FROM EVIL

LaShaun sat on the front pew and watched as Langston began to close his sermon. As he became more animated in his delivery, the musicians played lively, hitting the keys to accent every word.

He held the microphone and leaned backward, "Neither *death*... nor *life*..." he shouted before standing tall again.

"Angels...principalities... or *powers*..." He hit the podium.

"Nor things *present* or things to come, *church*..." He trotted to the right side of the pulpit and sang, "Nothinnng! Say *nothing* church!"

The church roared, "Nothing!"

He walked back to the podium enthusiastically. When he reached it, he looked at LaShaun as he lifted his handkerchief to wipe his forehead. She beamed as he winked at her.

Then he turned his attention to the congregation, pointing at various people in the pews. "Not you...you...you...or even me." He pointed to himself. "*Nothing* shall separate us from the love of God, which is in Christ Jesus." The musicians played softly.

"Do you believe that church?" The congregation responded affirmatively. Slowly, he turned the pages in his Bible, his chest rising and falling in quick succession.

"I don't care what you've done...or how far off course you've drifted. You can't *out-sin* God's love." He walked down three steps and stood on the bottom one. People all over the sanctuary stood. Some were crying, as others raised their hands in worship.

"My father used to say, 'God saves from the utter-most to the gutter-most.' And all you have to do is take Him at his Word and surrender your life to him. Is there one who wants to do that today?"

During Langston's appeal for salvation, LaShaun thought about the meeting she was having after church. She hadn't seen her old beau in ten years, and she knew soliciting his help could prove costly, but she had no other choice. She needed someone she could trust, who had no ties to Charlotte. Someone who loved her and would still, after all these years, do anything for her.

Following service, she slid out the side door of the sanctuary and hurried to her car. She had to drive to Dora's home, an hour away.

When Lucille died, Dora became her surrogate mother. And although she was aware of LaShaun's misdeeds, she never judged her. She gave her spiritual advice but allowed her to make her own choices.

When Langston proposed, Dora convinced her to accept it.

She has been his biggest proponent. And as her secretary, she keeps her eyes and ears open, notifying her of everything that goes down at DMI.

So, when she told Dora about Charlotte framing Karisma, she insisted LaShaun takes proactive measures to ensure her acquittal. Hence the reason for today's visit.

As she neared Dora's home, she received a call from Langston.

"Hi Babe, great service today," she answered cheerfully.

"Thanks, God was moving. Where are you? I thought maybe we could enjoy Sunday dinner together."

LaShaun nodded, regretful that she wouldn't be home until later. "Umm...Ms. Smith is under the weather, so I'm going to check on her. Do you mind eating a light lunch and we can go to dinner when I get back?" *Please forgive me for lying.*

"Ok, sure. I'll be here. Call me when you're on your way back, and I'll meet you somewhere."

"I will. Talk to you later." After they said their farewells, she ended the call. Ten minutes later, she was pulling into Dora's driveway.

When she unlocked the front door with her key and walked in, she was startled to see Monster on the sofa, drinking iced tea and watching television like he was the man of the house.

"Oh...hi," LaShaun said hesitantly. "I didn't expect to find you here already. Where's your car?" Her heart raced.

"Is that the way you greet someone after ten years?" He stood and held out his arms; she reluctantly walked into his embrace. His soft woodsy scent was intoxicating, and she stayed in his grasp longer than she should have. She hadn't been held in days, and she felt at home as her head lay against his thick, rock-hard body, and his muscular arms cradled her.

He was a professional bodyguard when she met him in college, and they had an instant connection. As she rode in the back of the limousine with her suitor, she would catch him sneaking glances. They became fast friends and, later, passionate lovers. They discussed marriage, but that dream ended when his wife ambushed them during one of their dinner dates. LaShaun immediately cut him off, but he stayed in touch with Dora.

Ten years ago, he faced a health crisis and LaShaun visited him in the hospital. He still expressed his undying love for her and apologized for not telling her he was married. And, thinking he might not survive his illness, she forgave him and acknowledged a part of her would always love him also. After she prayed for him, she laid on his chest and wept; for what they meant to each other, and for what could have been.

Fortunately, his health improved, and he now owns a cyber security firm. When she called him a week ago, it was as if no time had elapsed. They got into an easy rhythm and talked for hours. He informed her he'd divorced after his brush with death, but she wasn't surprised. Dora had informed her as soon as the ink was dry on the divorce decree.

Now, as he held onto her tightly, warmth electrified her body. She'd lost herself in his arms until Dora interrupted their reunion.

"Umm...hmm." She said playfully. "I knew I needed to make an appearance." She stood with her hands on her hips looking at them like she'd caught them on the brink of sin.

He quickly released LaShaun, and they all laughed awkwardly. LaShaun greeted Dora and hugged her. "Dinner will be ready soon," she said as she departed to the kitchen.

"How've you been?" Monster asked as LaShaun took a seat. Then he sat down.

"I've been good." She evaded his piercing brown eyes.

"This is me, Shaun. You can be real. I know you're not...*good*." He watched her fidget with her hands. "Is Langston treating you right?"

"Yes," she said quickly. "We're...we're good." He looked at her skeptically. "Ok," she conceded. "We're okay."

He smiled, and she chided herself for wanting to kiss his juicy lips. *Get a grip LaShaun.*

"So, tell me. Why am I here?" he asked pointedly.

She ran her fingers through her hair. "If you've been watching the news, you know what's going on at DMI." He shook his head affirmatively.

"I think the young girl that was arrested was framed by my partner," she told him.

"Charlotte?" He raised an eyebrow.

She nodded. "And I need to find out how she did it so that I can help the young lady get acquitted."

He clasped his hands and leaned forward. "That's heavy. What do you have to go on?"

"Not much. When I ask for details, she's evasive. That's why I need you."

"I need you too," he said seductively.

LaShaun laughed nervously and waved her hand. "Don't do that. I can't handle your advances right now." She tucked her hair behind her ears.

He chuckled in the way she always found sexy. "Fine. I'll leave you alone...for now."

She shook her head, and their eyes met. Feeling like a teenager with hormones running wild, she couldn't tear hers away. "Thank you," she managed to say.

"You're welcome." He rubbed his hands together. "Give me a week or so, and I'll have answers."

"Wow, that quick?"

"Yep. I'm handling this issue personally. And you can rest easy tonight...I got you." He licked his lips and smiled. She still found his bald head, dimpled cheeks, and clean-shaven face extremely attractive. He'd been the first man with light skin she'd ever fallen for.

"Dinner's ready," Dora announced. LaShaun was thankful to retreat from Monster's intense gaze. She hopped up and hurried to the kitchen– grateful for the food, Dora's company, and her watchful eyes.

When LaShaun called to let Langston know she was on her way home, he was at the hospital. A church member had been in a near-fatal car accident, and he was with the family. She was thankful to have time to go home and shower before seeing him. She didn't want to risk him smelling Monster's scent on her clothes.

When he finally made it home, she was in bed reading. The lamp on her nightstand was on to signify she was still awake. She heard him drop his keys on the kitchen counter and walk to the bedroom.

"Hey," he said as he stood in the doorway.

"Hey, how's the family?' she asked concerned.

"Hanging in there. How's Ms. Smith?" He stroked his goatee.

"She's better. Just a little bug." She took off her reading glasses. "Did you eat yet?"

"Of course. Our members had the hospital waiting room smelling like Popeye's." He chuckled lightheartedly.

She joined him. It had been a while since she'd seen him laugh so freely. She missed the easy way they engaged with each other. Remembering it, made her ashamed of the feelings that were roused with Monster.

"I'm going to watch a little television to wind down. We'll talk more in the morning. Good night." He turned to leave.

"Oh...okay. We'll talk tomorrow," she responded amiably.

After drifting off to sleep, she woke with her book sliding off the bed. She checked her phone - 3:00 a.m. Still groggy from sleep, she went into the den and found Langston snoring on the couch. One leg on the sofa and the other hanging off the side.

Shaking her head, she gently pulled his leg onto the sofa, then covered him with his favorite Steelers throw. She wanted to lay with him, to place her ear next to his heart so his steady beat could reassure her nothing had changed. But she couldn't bring herself to do it. She didn't know how he would react, and she couldn't face more rejection. After she turned off the television, she stood over him and prayed.

Lord, we need You now. Please help us find our way back to each other. Give us the courage to do what needs to be done, and please continue to show us Your love, mercy, and grace so that we can weather this storm. And Lord, please forgive me for my sins and cleanse me from all unrighteousness. In Jesus's name. Amen.

Chapter Nineteen
SURRENDER

Karisma sat in a tub of hot water, crying as droplets of blood rippled the water and disappeared without a trace. She'd done everything in her power to fight the urge to cut herself, but her addiction was at its strongest when she was at her weakest.

Her life was out of control, and she was slipping deeper into darkness. She could remove negative thoughts from her mind and chant affirmation for days, but neither had the power to grant her freedom. The kind of freedom she needed came solely through the shedding of blood. Her blood.

When she raised her left arm, three half-inch slits she'd carved on her forearm stared back at her. She smelled the blood clinging to her knife, but the cold steel hadn't provided the relief she so badly craved. So, the feeling of hopelessness and lack of control intensified.

Karisma closed her eyes, laid back against the tub, and knocked her head against the wall. Slowly at first, then quicker and harder.

When you're weak, that's when He's strong. When you're burdened, He wants to be your burden bearer. All you need is to invite Him in.

Karisma heard the words LaShaun had spoken at the women's conference so clearly. They didn't mean anything to her then, but now they pierced her soul. She snatched a towel from the side of the tub and buried her head in it, sobbing uncontrollably. Months ago, she didn't need or want God's help. Wanted nothing to do with Him. Now, God was the only one she felt could help.

Karisma was desperate for someone to take away the heartache, pain, and despair that was crushing her. She wondered if that someone was God. With a deep sigh, she willed herself to stop crying. "God if you're real, please send me a sign," she whimpered.

She took the washcloth and pressed it hard against the blood slowly trickling from her arm. After a few minutes, the bleeding stopped. Either she'd perfected the art of minimizing blood loss, or God was showing her mercy.

As she rose and placed one foot on the floor, there was a light tap on the door. "If you don't get out of that tub, you're going to turn into a prune," Deyja squeaked through the closed door. Karisma hated herself for causing the trepidation she detected in her mother's voice.

"I'm getting out now Mom," she called out.

"Okay. I was just checking on you."

Recently, Karisma heard Deyja telling her friend she lived with the constant debilitating fear that Karisma would start hurting herself again. She'd confessed that negative thoughts pervaded her mind and she had recurring dreams of finding Karisma in the bathtub lifeless. Karisma was afraid of the same thing.

When Karisma finally opened the door and stepped out, she

noticed Deyja trying to sneak a peek at her wrists, so she folded her arms as if keeping her towel from falling.

"Chamomile and peppermint tea is on the kitchen counter. Don't let it get cold." Deyja plastered on a fake smile.

"Thanks, Mom. You're the best!" Karisma scooted her body around Deyja and walked to her bedroom, careful not to draw more attention to herself.

Numb and mentally exhausted, she entered her room and dropped her towel on the floor. She would stay in her room until she was sure Deyja was no longer in the kitchen.

Her buzzing cell interrupted the breathing exercises she was doing under the ceiling fan's cool breeze to keep from cutting herself again. She intended to ignore it, but something pushed her to lean over to the nightstand and grab the phone.

"Hello, this is Karisma." She struggled to sound upbeat.

"Hi, Karisma! This is Heiress. How are you doing?"

Karisma's answer stuck at the base of her throat. She jammed a hand over her mouth to stifle her moans and put the phone on mute to keep Heiress from hearing.

"You were on my mind, so I wanted to reach out to you." Heiress said, oblivious that Karisma had muted her. "I can't hear you. I'm sorry - is this a bad time?"

Willing herself to respond, Karisma cleared her throat and took the phone off mute. "I'm fine," she croaked. "It's nice of you to call." She rose from her bed and slipped on her robe.

"Great! I wanted to know if you still need a lawyer to help with your…um…situation?"

"I'm not sure," Karisma confessed. "My parents are handling that, and they haven't said anything to me about it."

"Oh, okay."

Karisma started to say something but paused. She didn't want to think about the trial, but she didn't want to be rude to Heiress. Thankfully, Heiress changed the subject. "So, what have you been doing since we last spoke?" she asked.

"Not much. Just trying to figure out why my life is so crazy right now." Karisma sat on her bed and picked lint from her robe.

"I've been praying for you. I'm here if you need someone to talk to. I can't fathom what you're going through, but I can provide a listening ear if you need one." Heiress's voice was dripping in love. The sincerity she exuded prompted Karisma to open up to her.

"Heiress, I'm so overwhelmed," she gushed. "I'm putting emotional and financial stress on my parents, I was expelled from school, and I can't look at my phone or turn on the television without hearing what a horrible person I am. I just want this nightmare to be over. Do you think your mother can help me prove my innocence?"

"I can't promise you that, but I can say she's known as one of the best there is. Keep in mind the pandemic's going to determine how soon your case goes to trial. Judges are still postponing a lot of in-person hearings or conducting them through video conferencing."

Karisma slapped a hand on her forehead. "I don't want this cloud hanging over me indefinitely. It's ruining my life! Honestly, I don't know how long I can hold on. I'm struggling."

"I know it's hard, but God will never put more on you than you can bear," Heiress offered.

Karisma rolled her eyes. "I know you mean well, but I don't want to hear that. All that God talk doesn't encourage me. Besides, I don't even know what that means."

"What I'm saying is, God's not going to allow you to go through anything you can't handle. He will give you the strength to stand when you feel like falling. When the weight of the world is on your shoulders, He wants you to allow Him to carry it."

"That sounds good, but I have too much at stake here. My life is on the line!" She laid on her back and watched the ceiling fan rotate.

"That's the main reason you need to lean on Him. The heavier the load, the more you need Him to carry it. But your mind convinces you to rely on yourself or people because that's the only thing that makes sense to someone who doesn't have a relationship with Christ."

When Karisma didn't counter, Heiress kept talking. "As people, we all have limited resources, limited power, and limited ability to change anything. God alone, has all power. If you think otherwise, you're deceiving yourself."

I hear what you're saying, but I've never given God a second thought. I probably wouldn't be thinking about him now if I wasn't in this predicament. It would be hypocritical of me to suddenly give my life to Him. That's the ultimate jailhouse cliché.

"Your feelings are understandable. However, everyone will have a period of reckoning in life. A time when their situation is so dismal, and the stakes are so high, they can't see their way out. That's the time when they come to a crossroad and must decide whether to continue to go at it alone or trust in God."

Karisma quietly pondered Heiress's sentiments. Deep down in her spirit, she knew what her new friend told her was true, and she had to decide whether she would allow God in her life.

She turned onto her stomach. Her heart pounded, like the fist of God was knocking on it. *What do you have to lose? Trust Him.*

"How do I surrender to God when I'm not sure I even believe there is a God?"

"Trust me. If you didn't believe, you wouldn't be asking the question. Deep down, you know there is a God. You just haven't decided to give Him complete control over your life."

"How can you be so sure?"

"Because all humans are spiritual beings and all bow at the altar of something. For some it's the altar of money, it's power, for some it's drugs, sex, self, or any other vice that can seemingly help them through the journey of life. Everyone turns to something. You determine what that something will be."

"So, what do I do if I feel like that something could possibly be God?"

"Well, you can begin by learning more about Him and then make a decision about surrendering, or you can give up your desire to be in control and take a leap of faith."

Karisma's mind was warring against her. She truly wanted to take a leap of faith but felt like she needed to learn more about God first. Her mind raced through everything she'd ever heard about God. Much of it used to sound foolish to her, but after speaking to Heiress, it made more sense. She needed - and more importantly wanted, to surrender herself to God.

Karisma didn't know how long her decision-making process had taken, but it seemed like an eternity. Surprisingly, she still held her phone to her ear and Heiress was still on the other end.

"Heiress, are you still there?" Karisma asked.

"Yes, I'm here. Are you okay?"

"I'm just thinking...I want to learn more about God." After waiting a few seconds, she blew out a slow breath and added cautiously, "I want to start by taking a leap of faith."

"Yessss!" Heiress screamed on the other end, making Karisma laugh. She didn't know what she was feeling, but she knew she'd never felt it before now.

Once Heiress calmed down she said, "I'm so happy for you, Karisma! Do you want to pray the prayer of salvation with me?"

"Yes, I think so," Karisma answered without hesitating.

"Repeat after me," Heiress directed.

"Dear Lord, I am a sinner in need of Your grace. Lord, I believe in You and your Son, Jesus. I believe He died for my sins, rose for my justification, and now sits at Your right hand, making intercession on my behalf. Lord, I surrender my life to You, and I vow to study your Word and live by Your standards. In the name of Jesus, I pray, Amen."

When they were done praying, neither woman spoke.

...they were too busy rejoicing.

Chapter Twenty
OPENED DOOR

Heiress and Johnysa sat on the back deck of Johnysa's home, sipping tea and gazing at the serene blue water beckoning them to take a swim. Spring had come on the scene like a runway model, and its beauty was on full display. The cool waters would be soothing, but neither of them wanted to jump in the pool and mess up their freshly coiffed weaves.

Johnysa had just won a contentious, high-profile divorce and the mayor's wife dubbed her *The Divorce Diva*. Ever since she made her proclamation on the evening news, Johnysa's phone had been ringing off the hook.

Heiress admired her mother and was excited when Johnysa took the day off and invited her to "self-care day." She didn't look like she was in her early fifties, more like her early forties. Clad in a cream lounge set, flawless makeup, and hair pulled back into a long braid, girls half her age couldn't hold a candle to her.

She glowed as she brought Heiress up to date on the latest news of her divorce. It became final two weeks ago, and the judge awarded her everything she wanted: the house, half her now ex-husband's retirement, and several shares of stock.

She laughed hysterically as she mimicked the look of horror on "the bastard's" face when the judge awarded alimony to his already generous ruling. If Heiress hadn't known better, she would've bet Johnysa faked depression and closed her practice so "the bastard" would have to pay her indefinitely. That would stick it to him and the young, soon-to-be Mrs. Storm, the second.

"I'm representing Karisma," Johnysa casually revealed over lunch. "Normally, I wouldn't be sharing this with you, but in this case, I've been granted permission."

Heiress clapped her hands in delight. "That's fantastic, Mom! If anyone can prove Karisma's innocence, it's you."

"I can't guarantee anything, but the state's case is extremely weak. It won't be a slam dunk by any means, but I think we have a decent chance of getting her acquitted. And I won't tell you anything else, so don't ask," Johnysa admonished with a huge smile.

Her love for practicing law showed on her content face. Heiress knew her mother needed the courtroom like a fish needs water. She'd told her many times that practicing was more therapeutic than therapy itself.

"I'm so happy you're doing better, Mom. I hated to see you so down."

Johnysa reached over and grabbed her hands. "Thank you, baby. It was a long, hard road, but God is faithful. I just had to remember

I was His child, and I had the victory over anything that came against me."

"Amen," Heiress said as she beamed proudly. They high-fived each other.

"What about you? What are you doing now that you've closed the store?"

"I'm not closed. I pivoted to an online shop, and it's doing well. It's doing so well, that I may never reopen the brick and mortar. Also, I've enrolled in a couple of online business classes to make up for what I don't know about marketing and accounting. I can't rely on social media to teach me everything." She giggled and lifted the cup of tea to her mouth.

Johnysa laughed also. "You'd swear TikTok was the Bible, girl. I have clients telling me how to do my job because of what they saw on that site. It's gonna have people in bad shape." She chomped on the almonds she'd been eating. "Did you apply for the Covid relief loan?"

"Yep. It was approved, and I'm waiting on a deposit now. I'm going to use it to buy out my lease and purchase new inventory. It will help me stay afloat while I determine my next move."

"I can help you make extra money while you decide," Johnysa offered nonchalantly.

Heiress eyed her mother suspiciously. "Doing what?"

"The pandemic is causing my caseload to increase faster than I can keep up, and I need help keeping my files in order, responding to correspondence, and maintaining other light office duties. I may also need you to go to the courthouse to file documents from time to time."

Heiress pushed out a heavy sigh. Johnysa had always wanted her to become a lawyer so they could open a firm together. Heiress was interested in law but ultimately decided against it. Johnysa would never see her as an equal, and Heiress couldn't see herself under her mother's overbearing control indefinitely. Just like she did everything else in Heiress's life, Johnysa would second-guess every decision she made.

"I don't know, Mom. I think it would be better if you hired someone else."

"Why would I do that? You are fully capable, and I can trust you." Johnysa took a deep breath and leaned back in her seat with a smirk. "Listen, I'm not at a place where I can trust anyone I don't know. And besides, why should I give money to a stranger when my daughter can benefit from it?"

Heiress closed her eyes and shook her head. She knew she'd never find a way to turn Johnysa down. "I'll help you for three hours per day, no more," she reluctantly agreed. "I still have a business to run, and I have to perform well in my classes."

"Agreed," Johnysa said with a wide grin.

"Stop all that cheesing. When the pandemic is over, you have to find someone else," Heiress kidded.

"I'll take that." Johnysa grabbed her teacup. "Your first order of business is getting me added to LaShaun's calendar."

Heiress shook her head in disbelief and threw her napkin at her. "I'm already regretting my decision," she said playfully. Johnysa laughed and rose to give her a bear hug. When she returned to her seat, they sat in comfortable silence.

"Well since I'm on the case," Heiress broke the silence, "I have some information that could be helpful.

Johnysa's eyes had been closed, so she opened them and turned her head towards Heiress. "What is it?"

"I ran into Karisma's roommate a few days ago and get this... she says she and Karisma were at an Alpha party the night the police alleged Karisma was seen leaving the hotel. According to her, Karisma was pretty wasted when the party ended, and her roommate drove her back to her apartment."

"What's the roommate's name?"

Visibly irritated by the disruption, Heiress responded, "Her name is Makayla. I don't know her last name. But anyway, she's not sure what time they left, but it was well after one."

"And she stayed at the apartment all night?".

"That's the problem," Heiress answered. "She spent the night with her boyfriend, so she can't say for sure." Putting up her pointer finger, she added, "*But...* Karisma didn't have her car and, even if she did, she was too drunk to drive. Makayla says her boyfriend had to carry her to the room and put her in bed."

"Okay, that could help raise reasonable doubt. Why hasn't she gone to the police?"

Heiress shrugged. "She didn't want to be involved, I guess. Why hasn't Karisma said anything?"

"I don't know," Johnysa answered as she rose from her seat to enter the house. "But I intend to find out."

Two days later, Heiress knocked on the front door of LaShaun's home, with Johnysa by her side. The door opened, and they were greeted by Rosa. After pleasantries were exchanged, she escorted them through the foyer to a large room with an elegantly dressed seating area to the left, a round glass table with eight fancy chairs in the center, and a palatial kitchen to the right.

Heiress had been there many times before and knew her way around well. Caleb-LaShaun's chef was cooking gumbo and Heiress introduced him to Johnysa. Then they both sat at the table and waited for LaShaun. The aroma emanating from the sausage, shrimp, spices, and other ingredients made their stomachs growl and mouths salivate.

Johnysa shared that during college, she and LaShaun would frequent a local restaurant specializing in New Orleans Creole Gumbo. They laughed as she told Heiress how the two of them would sit on her bed at three o'clock in the morning devouring leftovers they'd vowed to save for their next day's lunch.

"What are you two cackling about?" LaShaun asked pleasantly as she entered the room and reached down to give them both a hug. Heiress hugged freely and pecked her on the cheek. Johnysa stiffened and responded professionally, "Hello, Mrs. Delaney. Thank you for agreeing to meet with me."

LaShaun sat across from her and waved her hand. Snarkily, she responded, "I know we haven't spoken in a long time, but it ain't all that. You can still call me LaShaun."

Figuring it was best to stay out of it, Heiress remained quiet. Johnysa replied, "As you wish. Thanks for meeting with me-*LaShaun*."

Smiling, LaShaun replied, "I was happy to." She looked as if she was seeing Johnysa for the first time. "You haven't changed a bit, and Heiress looks just like you. She's smart like you too," she added.

Fighting the urge to come back with a snide comment, she responded, "Thank you. "You haven't changed either."

Heiress recognized the double entendre and cut in immediately. "Why haven't you ever said anything about the gumbo you and my mom couldn't get enough of?"

LaShaun smiled, "I just assumed your mom told you."

Heiress looked between the two of them. "Nope. For some

reason, y'all don't want to share details about your college days. I'm starting to think y'all killed somebody."

LaShaun laughed, and Johnysa took her pad and pen from her large purse, ignoring the exchange.

As Caleb placed a small charcuterie board and pitcher of mango tea in the center of the table, LaShaun dismissed him for the night. He responded that the gumbo was simmering, and told them all to enjoy the rest of their evening.

After he left, they got down to business. Heiress remained quiet and took notes as her mom conducted the interview.

LaShaun was very forthcoming with information and adamant in her belief that Karisma was innocent of the charges. Johnysa asked LaShaun whether she knew of a reason anyone would want to frame Karisma. She noticed a slight hesitation as LaShaun answered, "Definitely not." She also noted how LaShaun raked her fingers through her hair and pinned it behind her ears, her tell.

"You're not being honest with me," Johnysa said. Heiress gawked at her, startled.

"Excuse me?" LaShaun responded, feigning indignation.

Johnysa stared at her and pursed her lips before answering. "I've known you for years, and you always mess with your hair when you're lying or withholding information. So, speak truthfully or don't speak at all."

Heiress released the breath she'd been holding when LaShaun shook her head and blushed.

"Karisma had nothing to do with Deacon Thomas's death. She does not work for Sweet Dreams Boutique, and I am not a madam. You must do everything in your power to prove that to a jury," LaShaun stated emphatically.

Johnysa paused before responding. "Thankfully, I don't have to prove anything. That's the prosecutor's job. All I need to do is raise reasonable doubt. How can you help me do that?"

LaShaun thought for a moment. She couldn't tell her what Charlotte had done, but she refused to sit by and let Karisma take the fall. "I'm not sure, but I'll do what I can. If you need private investigators, a forensics team, or another autopsy, let me know. I don't want you to cut corners because of money."

Deyja sat back and crossed her arms. "I appreciate the offer, but it would be unethical and a conflict of interest for me to take money from you to aid in Karisma's defense. However, I'm still in the early stages of my investigation, so I may have to call you and follow up from time to time. You have my number. If you think of anything to add, please give me a call."

"I will," LaShaun answered. Heiress will give you all my contact information. And if that's all, let's share some gumbo for old time's sake."

Johnysa responded politely. "No thanks. I have another interview right after this, so we better get going."

"I'll take some for the road," Heiress said as she got up and walked to the kitchen.

"I knew you wouldn't pass up food," LaShaun teased. "How you stay so tiny, I'll never know." She walked over to Heiress and put an arm around her shoulders. Johnysa watched them with fire in her eyes.

After LaShaun gave Heiress enough gumbo for five people, she walked them to the door. Before she opened it, she turned to face Johnysa and opened her arms wide. Reluctantly, Johnysa walked into her embrace. As they held each other closely, she whispered, "Thanks for your help." LaShaun nodded her head up and down and responded, "My pleasure."

As they drove away, LaShaun wondered what her life would be like had they remained friends. Johnysa, cruising down the driveway in her new Polar White Mercedes EQS Sedan, wondered the same thing.

Chapter Twenty-One
AIN'T NOTHING FREE

LaShaun felt a showdown was on the horizon. One day Langston was fine. The next day he avoided her like she was infected with COVID-19. Most days, he left before she woke up and returned after she'd gone to bed. On other days he stalked around the house slamming doors or playing gospel music loud enough to wake the dead.

Dora informed her that some members of the congregation thought he should step down until everything blew over. More importantly, one of his associate ministers was lobbying behind his back, wanting to be the interim pastor.

Although she knew Langston was under a lot of pressure, she was fed up with him teetering between hot and cold. She'd rather him pick a side, so she'd know whom she was getting each day. So, she'd made up her mind to force him into a conversation.

Last night, she directed Rosa to wake her as soon as he left for his morning run. Rosa did as she was told, and LaShaun posted in the mudroom waiting when Langston returned.

"We need to talk," she snapped as soon as he walked in the door.

"I don't have time t--"

"Make time! You're not leaving this house until we have this conversation."

He took off his running shoes. "You are in no position to tell me what I'm not doing." Langston's chest swelled with anger.

"There's *no* position higher than a wife, and you will find yourself without one if we don't talk." She refused to back down.

Langston was incredulous. "Are you threatening me?"

"I do not need to threaten you. I'm stating facts," LaShaun coolly uttered. "If you don't want me, leave. But if you do, we need to work this out today. I can't fight the press, church folk, *and* you."

Langston huffed. Hating confrontation, he acquiesced. "Can I shower first?"

"Sure," LaShaun responded softly and sulked to the kitchen.

While she waited for Langston, she whipped up turkey bacon, scrambled eggs, cheese grits, and toast. Langston returned just as she was squeezing fresh orange juice.

Over the years, she found that conversations over meals were less volatile and yielded a higher chance for resolution. She prayed that proved true today.

"Where's Rosa?" Langston pulled a stool out from the island and plopped down.

"I gave her the morning off. She'll be back after her doctor's appointment."

Neither of them wanted to speak first. They kept their heads down in awkward silence as they ate, staring at their plates or anywhere else but each other.

Alright, looks like I need to make the first move. "Langston..."

"Yes," he mumbled without looking up.

LaShaun rolled her eyes but refused to be deterred. "I'm sorry to have brought such scrutiny on the church and us. What can I do to fix this?"

"Telling the truth would be a good start." Finally, Langston lifted his head, peering into her eyes.

"Why do you think I'm not?" she asked, still feigning innocence.

He slammed his hands on the island and hopped up. "Because I'm not a fool!"

LaShaun was taken aback by his outburst and didn't want to make matters worse.

"I'm not saying you are," she said to placate him. "But what do you think I'm lying about?"

"Everything! And I've avoided having this conversation with you because I knew it would be difficult. I know you're lying, and I don't know how to handle your dishonesty. I know you feel like you can't tell me the truth and it tears me apart." He sat down and stabbed his eggs with his fork.

"Some days I want to hold you and tell you everything will be okay...that I'll make sure of it. But that would only empower you to continue the lie. My heart is hurting because in all our years together, this is the first time I've felt like I don't know you at all." He put the fork down and folded his arms, love, and concern still in his eyes.

LaShaun knew at that moment that if she didn't trust him and lay it all on the table, she'd lose him for sure. She couldn't protect him or their marriage by withholding the truth, so she said a quick prayer and cleared her throat before diving in.

"When I met Charlotte, she was everything I was not." The words slipped off her tongue, and she didn't hold them back.

"We came from a similar background, but she was more sophisticated than I was. Always rocking the latest fashions, had her own car. She was street-smart, bold, and cunning. To me, there was nothing she lacked. And I lacked everything."

Langston remained quiet and waited for her to continue.

"Anyway, I was attending school on a scholarship, living on student loans, with no extra money for anything. My grandmother had died, and I was depressed, and sinking fast. I was determined to get my degree, and Charlotte threw me a lifeline."

LaShaun paused to study Langston, but she had a hard time reading his thoughts. Her hands shook as she gulped the rest of her juice, then continued.

"Charlotte and I were both pursuing business degrees and took a lot of the same classes. Soon, we began studying together, and a true friendship developed. At the beginning of our sophomore year, my scholarship was over, and I didn't have enough for tuition *and* room and board. But Charlotte had her own apartment and invited me to stay with her for free."

"Ain't nothing free," Langston interjected snidely. LaShaun didn't rebut him.

"Then, she confided in me. She told me how she was paying for her education and living expenses."

The vein in Langston's temples bulged from him gritting his teeth, and Lashaun wondered whether she should continue. As if reading her thoughts, Langston said, "Go on."

LaShaun continued, despite the fear rising within. "She told me she had a *benefactor*, and he financed everything for her." She kept her eyes on Langston to gauge his emotions, but he was stone-faced. She grabbed a paper napkin and twisted it as she kept going.

"I was still naïve at the time and had no idea what a *benefactor* was. When she explained it to me, I realized he was like most men I'd seen growing up. He was her sugar daddy. And she denied having sex with them. She convinced me they just wanted a pretty girl on their arms when they went to business and social engagements. Sometimes, she even accompanied them on trips."

Langston stopped biting his bottom lip and said, "What about you?"

Despite wanting to do the opposite, LaShaun pressed forward. "Please, let me get this out, and I promise all your questions will be answered." When Langston nodded, she moved on.

"One night, Charlotte was going to a Christmas party and asked me to go with her. I agreed. Her friend picked us up from her apartment, and I was his colleague's date for the evening. We had a nice time at the event, and we'd go out once or twice a month thereafter."

"Umph," Langston grunted. He crossed his leg and balled his fist as if trying to maintain control.

LaShaun sucked her teeth and continued. "There was no sex involved and I made more money than I would working a full-time job, so I didn't have a problem with it."

"Obviously," Langston nodded.

LaShaun ignored him and continued.

"After a few months, I was able to transfer to AU and stay in on-campus housing. By then, I was being paid to accompany men in their late fifties and early sixties who only wanted good conversation. Nothing more. They relished the fact younger men would envy them when they arrived at the party with someone young and pretty like me on their arm."

LaShaun took a deep breath. "One time, I went on a date with a very wealthy man. He was a black man, retired military, and a gentleman in every way. He wined and dined me, then took me back to campus. When I got out of the car, he asked to come inside to use the restroom. It was against the boundaries I'd set, but he'd been harmless all night, and I allowed it. He was intelligent, kind, and easygoing, so I let my guard down. When he finished using the restroom, we said our goodbyes, and I led him to the door."

She started trembling as she relived that moment.

"As I lifted my hand to unlock the deadbolt, he slammed me against the door and pinned me. I tried to fight him off, but he forced my dress up and jammed his hands into my underwear. I couldn't move. I...I...I tried to scream, but my face was pinned against the door, and all I could do was groan." She stared blankly into the distance.

"Then, he wrapped his arm around my waist and threw me onto the sofa. The impact knocked the wind out of me, and I knew resisting was futile...so I didn't.

He had his way with me...and all I could do was take it. After that, I felt like damaged goods. I didn't care about anything, so I continued going out. Only this time, I didn't say no to the ones who wanted sex. I just demanded they pay more money."

Her tears flowed freely as she kept her eyes glued to the floor. Langston rose from the table and paced back and forth. Then, he stopped pacing and doubled over as if he'd been gut punched. When she looked at him, he let out a thunderous roar.

He asked for the truth, and he got it.

Chapter Twenty-Two
THE NAKED TRUTH

"How long were you a prostitute?" Langston asked.

Seriously? I just bared my soul and told you I was raped, and this is what you ask me?

"I was an escort, not a prostitute," LaShaun defiantly insisted.

"Are you kidding me right now?" Langston shouted. "A woman who sells her body is a *pros-ti-tute. A fil-thy har-lot!*" Langston clapped his hands with every syllable. "Let's call a spade a spade."

She recoiled at Langston's belligerent outburst, even though what he said was true. She had been a prostitute, yet somehow, coming from his mouth it sounded even more salacious than it was. He said it with such disgust. Absolute vitriol. And it was too much to bear.

He walked over to the bay window and stood with both hands in his pockets.

"Is the boutique a front for an escort service?" Langston's voice was eerily calm.

LaShaun didn't answer, but she didn't need to. Her silence said it all.

"Well, I'll be damned," Langston said as he walked back to the island and gripped the quartz countertop. He bent forward and exhaled.

"You are everything I ever hoped for in a wife; smart...strong...supportive. A partner in every sense of the word. But I don't know you, do I?"

"You do know me. I haven't changed," she asserted.

"That might be the case. But you've hidden your *true* self from me. You've hidden the part that is capable of doing such...such..." He didn't finish his sentence. Instead, he sat across from her and studied her. Her face grew warm under his stare.

"How can you sit in church Wednesday after Wednesday, Sunday after Sunday, professing to love God when you run a prostitution ring?" Langston hissed. "And involving young girls, too? How do you do that...*First Lady.*"

"Hey, I'm helping those young women," LaShaun argued.

"Oh my God!" Langston bellowed loudly. "So, corrupting young, impressionable, girls is helping them? They don't realize the consequences of their decisions, but you do. Their misdeeds will follow them, and you, too." He stared at her with a look of disgust.

"You'd never understand," LaShaun retorted. "You've always had what you needed. You've never been alone, hungry, or broke. Things aren't always black and white, Langston. I know you think it is, but some people gotta make tough choices, choices they don't want to make. Choices they're forced to make. And my girls choose to have control over their own bodies. They *choose* a lifestyle that helps them attain a debt-free education while positioning themselves to be self-sufficient. And after college, they have an opportunity to create generational wealth."

"Don't give me that!" Langston shouted with both hands in the air. "Is that really your excuse to justify what you're doing?"

"Like I said...You'll never understand," she said defiantly. They stared at each other, neither willing to look away first.

"You will relinquish your ownership in that...that...whorehouse," he demanded as he jabbed the table with his finger. "What you do is a slap in my face and a disservice to God. It ends today."

LaShaun opened her mouth to protest but said nothing. He'd made his position clear, and the ball was in her court. Langston rose from the table and strolled out of the room without another word.

LaShaun was still at the table when he returned and gathered his keys and messenger bag. There were no tears left to cry. Not even when Langston's footsteps faded as he went out the door, the car cranked, and she heard him pull out of the driveway.

LaShaun immediately called Dora.

"Hi, how are you this morning?" LaShaun asked when she picked up on the second ring.

"I'm fine. How are you?"

"I'm good." She said sluggishly.

"Why call if you're gonna lie," she chuckled. "It's in your voice. What's wrong?"

"Langston finally knows the truth," LaShaun answered wearily. "And he has ordered me to relinquish my share of the business."

"As he should have. I told you this day was gone come, chile. I hope you will listen to him because you sure won't listen to me."

"I do listen, but I also bear the burden of protecting those girls. How do I weigh what's best for me against what's best for them? I know what will happen to them if Charlotte has only herself to answer to. She's not going to look out for their best interest. She looks out for the ones putting money in her pockets. To her, the girls are dispensable and easily replaceable."

"I know you think you're doing the right thing. And it's wonderful you want to help them girls, but there are other ways to do it. You and Langston have enough money to fund a foundation, send hundreds of students to college, any number of things."

"I hear you, but it's not that simple. I must protect these girls and help them have the life God has for them. I know that is my calling."

"Baby, you're in a war between the sacred and profane. You're trying to do right by doing wrong! And that never ends well. You've been deceiving your husband, blaspheming God, promoting lewdness and all manner of evil. To top it off, you've fooled yourself into thinking you're doing what God has called you to do. It's all good until it's not."

LaShaun sat quietly and held the phone. This entire time, she'd convinced herself that she wasn't in the business for self-gain. The original plan was to get in and get out, but years later, the boutique was still open for business. "How did I end up *here?*" she asked.

"You're a good woman with a heart of gold," Dora consoled, "but it's time for you to stop kicking it with the devil. And she calls herself Charlotte."

LaShaun giggled despite her inner turmoil. "You know what, I can't with you."

"You know it's true. Charlotte has no use for the things of God, and you have no business yoking yourself to her. It's time to cut ties, and you know it."

"But she has always looked out for me. I wouldn't be here without her."

"That's a lie from the pits of hell! You wouldn't be here without God. He was taking care of you long before you knew there was a Charlotte. He sent Langston to find you. Charlotte had nothing to do with that. He's given you the brains, the fortitude, and everything you need to be right where you are, without casting your morals aside. And it's blasphemous to give the credit to anyone else, especially the devil in disguise."

LaShaun could tell Dora was worked up. She didn't play about giving man glory for God's goodness. "Calm down. I didn't mean to discount who God is in my life and what He means to me. I'm just saying, Charlotte was there for me when no one else was."

"And she was sent by the enemy to lead you astray, and you followed blindly. But you aren't blind anymore. It's time to decide. How you gonna live the rest of yo' days?"

"That's a good question," Lashaun responded softly.

"And you already know the answer," Dora said lovingly. "It's not easy, but it's necessary. And you know I'm gonna stick beside you through thick and thin. And that is *my* calling."

"You're right. I have some soul searching to do. And the time has come for Charlotte and me to part ways."

"Amen to that," Dora responded. *Amen* to that.

Chapter Twenty-Three
THE ASSIGNMENT

LaShaun tossed and turned all night. She woke up with a massive headache and her stomach in knots, but despite the pain, she had an assignment: Secure Karisma's acquittal and sever ties with Charlotte.

Langston's ultimatum put LaShaun in an extremely dangerous position. There was no way to get out without stabbing Charlotte in the back. If she were going to get out alive, she'd have to move strategically and keep Charlotte in the dark until it was done.

First, she needed valuable intel from Johnysa. She was close to the case and would know what type of evidence the district attorney was planning to use against Karisma. Evidence Charlotte, no doubt, planted.

In return, LaShaun would help to get Karisma off and take Charlotte down at the same time. It was the only way to defeat the true mastermind behind the operation and beat Charlotte at her own game.

LaShaun sent Heiress a text message. **Are you free for lunch? Sure, what time? I have an appointment at two. 11:30. Meet me at Bistro**.

Bistro was an upscale restaurant overlooking LaShaun's neighborhood golf course. It was quiet, elite, and discreet enough to discuss sensitive matters. Patrons were too busy handling their own business to pay attention to anyone else's.

LaShaun arrived early and was seated at her favorite patio table. She ordered a ginger ale for herself and water for Heiress. While she waited, she watched a group of women playing the 18th hole.

A million thoughts about how her plan could go south swirled through her mind. As Johnysa's assistant, using Heiress to feed her confidential information about the case was a breach of attorney-client privilege, and could jeopardize Johnysa's license to practice. It was a tremendous risk, but there was no way around it. LaShaun was asking the impossible, but she pushed the thought aside to focus on the greater good.

Heiress arrived at 11:30 on the dot. LaShaun loved that she was a stickler for arriving on time, like herself. She stood and gave her a huge hug. Although they wore masks, she was careful to turn her face away from Heiress's.

Once seated, they scanned the table's QR code and opened their Bistro app. While they waited on their food, LaShaun pivoted to the reason she requested the lunch meeting.

"I've spent the last few days trying to figure out how I can help Karisma beat her charges. Have you spoken with her lately?"

"I saw her at the Motion to Suppress hearing, but we didn't get a chance to talk."

"Was the motion successful?"

"Nope. The judge ruled the search warrant was valid and properly executed, so the evidence obtained from her dorm room can be admitted into evidence at trial," Heiress said morosely.

"That's a tough break." LaShaun's hands were steepled beneath her chin.

"It is, but not exactly a surprise. It's an election year, and the judge is trying to score points. He's pandering to conservative voters."

"It's going to be difficult getting an acquittal. What are the odds of winning?"

"It's starting to look grim. Karisma's family can't afford private investigators or medical experts, but my mom's optimistic."

"You know, with the right information, I can get our private investigator to do some digging to disprove the evidence against Karisma or get enough to raise reasonable doubt to get her acquitted. I have access to the assistant medical examiner too in case you need me to contact her for anything."

Heiress shook her head. "That would be great, but I don't think my mother wants you anywhere near this case. And I'm positive Mrs. Stanley's dead set against it."

LaShaun leaned forward and lowered her voice. "Well, what if my involvement stayed between you and me? You let me know the specifics and what you need help with, and I'll help you get around the roadblocks."

Heiress's antenna went up, and she looked at LaShaun suspiciously.

LaShaun sensed Heiress's hesitancy. "Listen, I know this sounds crazy, but I want to help Karisma get out of this mess. I've always believed in her innocence, and I won't rest until she is acquitted." When Heiress didn't respond, LaShaun fought harder. "You know me Heiress, and you know I have your and Karisma's best interest at heart. Please, let me help."

"I hear what you're saying, but I can't betray my mom's confidence. Let me tell her what you're proposing, and maybe she can think of ways to use your help without divulging sensitive information that can get her in trouble."

"That's just it - I can't help without confidential information. Your mother's made it clear that she wants nothing to do with me, so it's best if I work behind the scenes. You and I both know Johnysa, and I can't work together."

Heiress nodded. "True, but Mom's hands are tied. I know she wants what's best for Karisma, so she may be open to anything. Even if anything means working with you."

Later that evening. Heiress arranged for LaShaun to visit Johnysa at her home. When the door opened, Johnysa held it ajar and, with unbridled disdain, said, "Come in?"

"Thank you," LaShaun responded politely. Johnysa directed her to a small office a few feet from the door. She sat at the chair closest to the door, and Johnysa sat on the opposite side of the desk, facing her.

"Look," Johnysa began. "I took this meeting as a courtesy to Heiress, but I can tell you...I don't think there's any way we can work on this case together."

LaShaun cocked her head to the side. "Can you put up the daggers for one moment? I'm not your adversary."

"I'm not so sure of that," Johnysa stated emphatically. "You proved a long time ago you can't be trusted."

LaShaun was thrown by the statement. Furrowing her brow, she asked, "When? I've never done anything to you."

Johnysa hadn't planned to discuss the past, but the door was open, and she was marching in.

"You were my best friend. We did everything together. Then, after I gave birth to Heiress and got married, you ghosted me. You skipped my mother's funeral after claiming to love her so much, then left your godchild and me behind. Then, when we finally spoke, you lied about why you left. I'm not bringing this up because I want to restore our relationship. I want you to understand why I can't trust you."

"I get that. I was wrong, and I'm sorry."

Johnysa was visibly irritated. "You're still skirting the issue instead of telling me the truth about what happened so I can gain some clarity. You want to apologize and expect me to move on, but I can't. Not until I know the truth."

LaShaun didn't want to have this conversation either. She'd buried the past long ago. However, she knew she wouldn't get anywhere unless she spoke up. Johnysa was not going to bulge otherwise. She placed her purse on the empty chair next to her and dove in.

"You're right. You and I were like family. I loved you and Heiress, and leaving you ripped me apart. But continuing our relationship was too painful. When I left, I thought I was acting in everyone's best interest."

Once again, truth knocked at the door and demanded entrance. LaShaun couldn't outrun it any longer. If the truth could make her free *and* lead to a possible reconciliation, it had to be told. She interlaced her hands, took a deep breath, and revealed the reason behind her abrupt exit so long ago.

"When I met Hamilton, I couldn't put my finger on it, but there was something about him that unsettled me. You were happier than I'd ever seen you, he was doing a great job stepping up to take care of Heiress, and you got engaged. I didn't have any reason to believe he wasn't legit, so I didn't want to do anything to stand in your way."

"I wish you had," Johnysa blurted jokingly. LaShaun smiled.

"Our senior year of college, you and our sorors went to Miami for spring break. I stayed behind to work." She hesitated and bit her bottom lip. "I've never admitted it, but I was working as an escort." Johnysa open her mouth to speak and LaShaun held up a palm to stop her. "We can talk about that later. Right now, I need to get through this. Long story short, I was raped."

Johnysa gasped and placed both hands over her mouth.

"It's okay. God has given me peace about it, and I've moved forward."

Johnysa's eyes were wide. "I'm so sorry! I knew you changed after that night, but I never expected..." She shook her head as if that could erase the pain of the past.

"You had no reason to suspect it. I did everything in my power to remain normal. I put it in a box and focused on graduation. Shortly after, I found out I was pregnant."

"What are you saying?" Johnysa asked cautiously.

"After graduation, I went away so I could give birth without anyone knowing. It was a girl." LaShaun released a sad, long sigh. "My baby was adopted, and for my sanity's sake, I refused to look back.

Fast forward two years, and it's your wedding day. At the reception, you introduced me to Hamilton's fraternal twin - and I was looking into the eyes of the man who raped me."

Chapter Twenty-Four
A PATH TO VICTORY

Johnysa rose from her chair and hugged LaShaun. "I'm so sorry, Shaun." She grabbed her hands. "Let's go into the living room to talk." LaShaun Followed her.

When they sat on the oversized tan leather couch, Johnysa spoke first.

"For years, I believed you and Hamilton betrayed me. I even played love scenes in my mind and envisioned your bodies intertwined many times. I saw the weird chemistry between you two, and I scripted an award-winning movie in my head. And I convinced myself God had revealed it to me. I can't believe I was so foolish."

LaShaun grabbed her hand. "You were not foolish. I could have handled things better, but I didn't want to ruin your relationship with Hamilton or Heiress's future. I'm sorry."

Johnysa smiled wholeheartedly. "Apology accepted. I'm just glad I know the truth."

LaShaun put her hand to her hair, then took it down quickly.

"Spill it," Johnysa demanded.

Since Langston knew the truth, she decided to confess to Johnysa as well.

"Sweet Dreams Boutique is an undercover sex ring."

Johnysa harrumphed and waved her hand. "Girl, tell me something I don't already know."

LaShaun was flabbergasted. "What do you mean you already know?"

Johnysa nodded. "That fact's been circling the courthouse for years. Any lawyer worth his salt knows at least one judge, police commissioner, or councilman, connected with that boutique of yours."

"Okay. How do you feel about that?" LaShaun asked cautiously.

"Well...I've known you for a long time, and I believe your heart is in the right place. So, I hope you will go legit one day. I want you to practice what you preach."

"Ouch!" LaShaun responded.

Johnysa gave her a genuine hug, and LaShaun reciprocated. The rest of the night they discussed their heartaches and disappointments...victories and triumphs. They cried, laughed, and cried some more, attempting to recreate memories stolen by years of manufactured lies, secrecy, and distrust.

Before LaShaun left for the evening, they agreed to meet the following night to develop a plan to help Karisma beat the charges against her.

LaShaun and Heiress arrived at Johnysa's at six o'clock, and they immediately got down to business. As they ate pizza and drank soda, they poured over the details they already knew.

Johnysa pulled out the Incident Report from December 19, 2019. "It says here that Deacon Thomas dialed 911 at 12:25 am," Johnysa began.

"Or the person in the room with him could have done it before she fled," LaShaun offered.

Johnysa glared at her. "Let's stop it with *somebody*," she said using air quotes. "You know her name. What is it?"

LaShaun rolled her eyes and groaned. "Fine. It's Claudia. And yes, she's a Dream Girl."

Heiress laughed at the two of them. Johnysa agreed not to share with Heiress any of the information she'd learned the night before.

"Moving along," Johnysa continued. "When paramedics arrived, he had a faint pulse but coded twice en route to the hospital. A statement from the hotel manager revealed he'd checked into the hotel at 6:30 pm, had a meal in the hotel's restaurant, and entered his room at 8:17."

"And his female guest arrived at 9:47 in a long, black, hooded coat. So that can be anybody," Heiress surmised. She looked at Johnysa, who nodded in agreement.

"And at 12:26 am, right after the phone call, she left the room and used the back stairwell to exit the building," LaShaun added. "And I know from his children his pacemaker gave out at the hotel, which caused him to pass out."

"He died on top of me," Johnysa playfully mimicked a line from *The Color Purple*. She and Heiress burst out laughing, and LaShaun swatted them both. "You should be ashamed of yourselves," she admonished playfully.

"We're sorry," Johnysa giggled as she picked up another document. "So, the prosecutor's theory is that he had a heart attack in the hotel, and then Karisma came to his hospital room to finish the job so that she can cover up her illegal activities."

"And the police truly believe Sweet Dreams Boutique is an undercover sex ring that gets its girls from AU," Heiress interjected. "Detective Cruz does especially."

"Hmph," LaShaun responded. Her face contorted.

"What's wrong?" Heiress and Johnysa asked in unison.

"Are you referring to Victor Cruz?" she asked Heiress.

"Yes," Heiress answered cautiously. "Why?"

"Vic is one of Charlotte's eyes and ears on the force."

Heiress's heart dropped, and she tried to steady her voice. "Vic works for Charlotte? Are you sure?"

"Absolutely. He has for years."

"Describe him," Heiress challenged. "The Vic I'm referring to seems above-board."

"That's the point," LaShaun countered. "No one is supposed to *know* you're on the take."

Heiress held her tongue. Her face was flushed, and tears pooled in the bed of her lower eyelids.

"Are you okay?" Johnysa asked.

"I'm fine," Heiress said as she rose from the floor and fled to the bathroom. LaShaun and Johnysa stared at each other, perplexed.

"Did I miss something?" LaShaun asked.

"Right after you mentioned knowing Detective Cruz, she looked like she'd seen a ghost," Johnysa observed.

"You think there's something she isn't telling us?"

"I don't think so. What could she be hiding?"

"I don't know, but sickness like that doesn't creep up on you unless you've received news you don't want to hear, or you're pregnant."

"Or both," Johnysa added as she looked in the direction of the bathroom. Soon, they heard her regurgitating and rushed to the door. Heiress had forgotten to lock it and they barged in.

Johnysa grabbed a face cloth and wet it to wipe her face. LaShaun located the mop, so she could clean the floor. Then, they returned to the living room while Heiress showered.

When she rejoined them, crackers and ginger ale were waiting on her.

"Are you okay, sweetie?" Johnysa asked when she ate the last cracker.

"Yes ma'am," Heiress responded dryly. "Vic and I are in a relationship," she blurted.

LaShaun and Johnysa gawked in disbelief.

"Don't act so surprised. I know you already figured it out. Especially you Momma."

"How long has this been going on?" Johnysa asked.

"Almost since the case was opened." Heiress began to weep and pulled a tissue from the pocket of her robe, then dried her eyes.

"Are you in love with him?" LaShaun asked.

Heiress nodded.

"And he claims to love you?" Johnysa asked, not as delicately as LaShaun.

"Yes."

Charlotte put him up to it," LaShaun said. "If he approached you when the case was still in its infancy, she wanted him to test how much you could be trusted. She was trying to see how much information you were willing to share with him."

"He asked about you during our initial interviews," Heiress

confirmed, "but I didn't have anything to tell him that wasn't public knowledge. You hardly ever came up again, and we rarely discuss the case now."

"I'm sure that's true. Otherwise, Charlotte wouldn't be so reserved." LaShaun looked to Johnysa. "What are we going to do now?"

"It depends," Johnysa answered, then turned to Heiress. "Are you going to confront him, or can we use this to our advantage?"

Heiress straightened up. "He's been using me, now it's time I use him."

LaShaun laughed heartily. "Girl if you don't look and sound like your momma! You are *definitely* her child."

Heiress was still hurting, but she managed to smile. Johnysa did also. Then she gave instructions.

"I need you to continue your relationship with Vic as if you aren't aware of his betrayal. Try to get as much information out of him as possible, especially about the investigation."

"How can I do that without him being suspicious."

"Don't do too much digging at one time, and don't initiate conversations. But when he opens the door, you walk in. You can figure out the rest."

Heiress nodded in agreement.

"And I will do the same with Charlotte," LaShaun informed. "She's been evading my questions, but I'm going to keep pushing her for information. And I'm also going to get a copy of the autopsy."

"And I will lay low. I want to lull the prosecutor into a false sense of security, then strike." LaShaun gave her a fist bump.

They each had their orders and, for the first time since accepting the case, everyone was on one accord, and Johnysa saw a clear path to victory.

Game on!

Chapter Twenty-Five
A SMALL WIN

Two days after *Operation Freedom* was devised, LaShaun walked into Chateau Zen and checked in. She was scheduled for an hour massage and facial. While she was checking in, N'Kenge Sparks was in the locker room changing from her street clothes to a plush, white robe and slippers.

N'kenge is an expert DNA analyst and forensic pathologist, employed with the State Bureau of Investigation. She is one of nine medical examiners...and LaShaun's soror. Although she hadn't performed Deacon Thomas's autopsy, she has access to the results.

After securing her valuables in Locker No. 39, her masseuse led her to a dimly lit room where she would be wrapped in mud, scrubbed with aromatic sugar, and massaged so expertly she would have to force her body to leave the table.

As N'Kenge experienced restful bliss, LaShaun was escorted to the locker room. When the last spa goer exited, she went to locker number 39. Having received the code from Monster the night before, she input the digits, opened the locker, and retrieved a black, felt jewelry bag containing a black flash drive.

She now held the results of Deacon Thomas's autopsy, along with corresponding documents and an audio recording detailing the examiner's observation of every facet of the deacon's body...from head to toe, inward and outward.

LaShaun secured the small bag in her locker, exited the room, and was greeted by her awaiting therapist. She and N'Kenge would never cross paths.

On the way home, LaShaun called Charlotte and was sent straight to voicemail. Next, she called Langston. Again, voicemail. At lightning speed, her mood went from excited and relaxed, to agitated.

What is he doing that's so important he can't answer my call? She had taken an extended leave of absence from church duties but was tempted to drive by to see if he was there. *Nope. Won't do it. If he won't talk to me, I don't want to talk to him.*

According to GPS, she was forty minutes from her destination, just enough time to listen to Langston's latest sermon as she headed into the city. But before she pressed play, the phone rang. Thinking it was Charlotte or Langston, LaShaun didn't bother to look at the screen.

"Hello," LaShaun answered bubbly, not wanting to give either of them the satisfaction of knowing they'd gotten under her skin.

"Hello to you," Johnysa's voice chirped through the speaker. Even though they'd reconnected and called a truce, LaShaun was still shocked to hear her friend's voice. Johnysa hadn't called her in twelve years, or so. Sure, it wasn't a social call, but it was progress.

And it proved that on any day, at any moment, something special could take place.

"It's great to hear your voice," LaShaun admitted.

"It's nice to hear your voice, as well." Johnysa's cheerful voice quickly turned somber. "I have good news and bad news. Which do you want first?"

"Just let it do what it do," she said slangily. "I'm all ears."

"Roderick Butler's body was found in a landfill yesterday. His mother identified him this morning."

LaShaun wasn't sure what this meant to her. "I'm not familiar with that name. Who is he?"

"Karisma's cousin."

LaShaun sucked in air and blew it out before answering. "Oh, no! Are you serious?"

"That's not all. A young lady was found in the trunk of a burned car behind the Family Dollar in Stone Mountain. They retrieved the VIN from the engine block, and it was registered to Karisma's father. They may have found Karisma's car and our mystery girl."

"Nooo!" LaShaun screamed as she hit the steering wheel. "I pray it isn't her. Charlotte told me she'd sent her to Miami."

"I hate to say it, but Charlotte was probably lying. It's no coincidence that after months of searching, both were found the same day."

"I know. Someone is sending a message, but my heart breaks for their families." LaShaun said solemnly.

"Exactly. We need to figure out who's behind it. Did you get in touch with your private investigator?"

"Yes, I should receive a status report tomorrow. I also have the autopsy results, but I haven't viewed them."

"Yes," Johnysa shouted. "Can you come to the house so we can review the results together?"

"Let's meet at Bistro, where we'll be safer. It's at our clubhouse. I'm sending you directions right now."

"Don't bother. I've been there, and I vowed I'd never go back. That place was like the sunken place," Johnysa joked.

"Screw you," LaShaun chuckled. "Meet me there in an hour."

As soon as they hung up, LaShaun said a quick prayer for Rod, Claudia, and everyone involved in Karisma's case.

She called Charlotte again. Again, voicemail.

LaShaun decided against the sermon and drove to Bistro with the sounds of *Maverick City* ushering her into worship instead. She tried to shake Rod and Claudia from her mind; her own child was around their age. *I hope you're alive and well, she thought.* The alternative was too much to bear. Prayerfully, she'd done the right thing all those years ago.

As she entered Bistro, LaShaun glanced down for a moment to place her scarf in her purse and collided with Langston. He caught her before she hit the floor, looking at her with tender eyes. For a moment, the anger she'd seen every time her husband looked at her disappeared. She finally saw love in his eyes again.

He held her as she regained her balance and straightened up. "Thank you," she said as she hopped on one foot to a nearby chair. He made sure she was settled then said, "I'll be back."

She sat at a table for two while Langston said his goodbyes to the three gentlemen who accompanied him for lunch. While waiting, she retied the thin laces that curled around her legs. When she tightened them, she watched as Langston stood with his hands in his pockets, staring into the distance as his associates walked away. Then, dispassionately, he sauntered to the table and took a seat.

"I didn't expect to see you here," Langston said.

"I would have told you had you answered my call," LaShaun

responded. She hadn't meant to sound brash, but she couldn't help it. She was furious that he was out having fun with his friends instead of being miserable like her. He wasn't supposed to be able to eat, properly groom or string two sentences together. Yet here he was... handsome, smelling delicious, smiling and laughing while LaShaun was barely getting by."

"I'm sorry I didn't answer, but I haven't been in the headspace to speak with you," Langston confessed. "And I needed to be fully present for today's meeting. It was important."

"And I'm not?" LaShaun asked pitifully.

Langston reached across the table and held her hands in his. "Of course, you're important to me, you know that. But you also know we aren't in a good place. Let's not kid ourselves. I'm struggling, just like you are." He paused and stroked his closely cropped beard. "I'm prayerful, and I'm hopeful. But it's going to take a minute. It won't happen overnight."

"Do you still love me?" LaShaun asked.

"If I didn't, was it ever love in the first place?" Langston caressed LaShaun's hands before releasing them. She was relieved to hear him confess his continued love, and she understood his hesitancy. He needed time to fully process his emotions, just like her.

"I'm glad to hear I haven't lost you." LaShaun blinked back the tears threatening to fall from her eyes. "I'm doing everything I can to do what you've asked of me. That's the reason I'm here today. I'm meeting an old friend."

Langston raised a brow. LaShaun hadn't mentioned knowing Heiress's mother. She wasn't sure this was the time to bring it up, but since she was on a truth journey, she wasn't going to turn back. "Heiress's mother is my old friend. She's the lawyer representing Karisma, and I'm helping her with the case."

Alarm washed over Langston's face. "Why are you getting involved? Don't you have enough to worry about with the boutique?"

"It's a long story, and I promise you I'll answer all your questions, but I can't right now because Johnysa's on her way. Trust me, babe, this is the only way to get Charlotte out of our lives once and for all and identify Deacon Thomas's killer. I know I'm asking a lot but please, go with me on this. I'm doing this for us."

Langston didn't protest. When she set her mind to something, he couldn't change it. "Just be careful," he said.

"Thank you." LaShaun rose from her seat and kissed his cheek. Langston didn't flinch, but he didn't reciprocate, either. LaShaun was fine with that. The first step to a reconciliation was conversation. She considered their talk a small win.

Chapter Twenty-Six

CLEAN HANDS

As LaShaun sat at the Bistro waiting for Johnysa to arrive, she typed in Rod's name on her phone and clicked on the first item listed. It was a short blurb from the local newspaper.

Roderick Butler of 2222 Stanton Drive will be laid to rest on June 30, 2021, @ 2:00 pm, St. Rest Cemetery, 1630 Hwy.1, Sandersville, Georgia.

She was surprised that his entire life was reduced to twenty-four heartless, generic words. He didn't graduate high school, hadn't lived long enough to establish a career, didn't have a church home, and was unwed, and childless. All the things that make for a well-lived life. He had a grieving family who loved him, but no family members were listed.

Johnysa was escorted to her table by a waiter, and they ordered wine and an appetizer before he walked away.

Johnysa wasted no time bringing LaShaun up to date on what

she'd learned. She pulled out a stack of papers from her large purse and laid them on the table.

"I don't have long so we have to go through this quickly," she instructed.

"Ok, what is it?" LaShaun picked up the top sheet. Johnysa snatched it from her.

"I'm going to go over it, be patient," she scolded.

"I forgot how bossy you can be," LaShaun said while rolling her eyes. Johnysa laughed.

"I have a friend named Jorge who's a cyber security expert, and he came through big time," she said excitedly. Then she turned the sheet of paper towards LaShaun. "Somehow, he was able to use the VIN number from Karisma's car to hack into her GPS."

"It didn't burn up with the car?" LaShaun asked perplexed.

Johnysa stared at her like she had three eyes in her head. "The data is stored in the cloud, somewhere. And unless the cloud burns up, anything can be retrieved. Keep up."

LaShaun placed her hand against her chest. "Excuse me, Ma'am. I'll just shut up and let you talk."

Johnysa nodded playfully and pointed to the paper. "If you look at the timeline, it shows that at 11:22 pm on the night the deacon was rushed to the hospital, Karisma's GPS places her car at the club down the block. At 1:05, he arrived at Hampton Inn, where he stayed all night."

"So where was Claudia?"

"I don't know. Maybe he took her to the hotel."

"I'll tell my investigator to check into that."

"Ok, cool," Johnysa responded without looking up. "After check-out the next morning, he drove to Waffle House, an address on MLK Blvd, and then to the apartment he shared with his roommate, Jamal.

"How does Claudia know Rod? Do you know?"

"He didn't. He was a *Lyft* driver, and we're thinking Claudia flagged him down when she was leaving the hotel."

"Dang. So, he got mixed up in all this accidentally?"

"Yep. Wrong place at the wrong time." Johnysa added. "But this is where it gets interesting."

"You're really in your element," LaShaun marveled. "I can tell you're stoked by all this cloak and dagger business."

Johnysa winked and popped a fried asparagus stick in her mouth. Then she continued. LaShaun looked on in awe.

"Jorge was able to tap into his cell phone." She laid the top sheet to the side and picked up the second sheet. "At 5:45, he received a call that lasted 30 seconds. Then, at 6:00 pm, he received a text indicating his security alarm was tripped. A call from the monitoring service went unanswered and police were summoned to the residence."

"Did he call the police?"

"No. It appears he didn't respond, so the monitoring service requested a welfare check."

"Ok? So, what's the part that's interesting?" I don't need a play-by-play."

Johnysa shook her head. "You are so impatient." She picked up another asparagus stick. Chewing, she added, "That comes from not having to want for nothing. You expect everything to be quick, fast, and in a hurry,"

"Ok, Dr. Phil." She pointed at the paper. "Get to the good part."

"Right away your majesty," she joked. "They did the welfare check, and the place was empty. There was a sign of struggle, but since his cell phone and wallet weren't there, and neither was the vehicle neighbors say he often drove, the police chalked it up to sloppy housekeeping. The case was closed before it opened."

"So, you think someone kidnapped him?"

She wiggled her eyebrows. "I know someone kidnapped him."

"Who?" LaShaun asked excitedly.

"Charlotte. Well, one of her goons did it. And I think it was Cruz."

"You've got to be kidding." LaShaun shook her head in disbelief.

"I wish. At 7:30 pm, Rod's phone pinged off a tower near an abandoned warehouse in Forest Park. It went offline at 8:05, and never conveyed a signal again. Charlotte's cell phone pinged off the same tower around the same time, and so did Victor's."

She tossed the paper on the table like she was dropping a mic. "Charlotte either killed him or had him killed."

LaShaun's mind raced. "Why would she kill him?" She was livid that Charlotte would do this without clearing it with her first. "You should leak her actions to the police."

"I can't go to them with the illegally obtained information. We need to find something we can introduce in court. Any ideas?"

LaShaun rubbed her temples. "This is too much. Charlotte killed Rod. Did she also kill Claudia?" She looked at Johnysa for answers.'

Johnysa shrugged. "I have no idea. But if I were a betting person, I'd say yes."

"If we can't go to the police, what do we do with the information we have?"

"We use it as leverage when the time is right. Then we must get our hands on Cruz's cell phone and police log. I'm going to subpoena Rod's phone records since he's connected to the case."

"Okay. And I'm meeting with my investigator tomorrow. I'll let you know what I find out. In the meantime, we need to be careful."

"Yes, we do." Johnysa agreed.

LaShaun was so overwhelmed by what she'd heard that she didn't mention the autopsy. Instead, she ordered a meal to go, and they both agreed to talk later.

The next evening, LaShaun met with Monster. When she pulled up to Dora's, he was leaning against the passenger door of his car with his hands in his pockets. The serious look on his face suggested he was in a sour mood. He didn't move in her direction when she exited her vehicle, so she walked down the drive to meet him.

"Hi, what's wrong? You look distressed?" She hugged him.

"I'm good," he smiled. "Do you mind sitting in the car?"

"Why can't we go inside?" she asked suspiciously.

"Because I have an important meeting in an hour and if I go inside Ms. Dora will want me to stay and eat." He nodded towards the house, and Dora was in the window watching them.

"Fine. But you better be quick, or she will come out here to get us." She waved at Dora as Monster opened the car door for her.

"Nice ride," she commented when he sat in the driver's seat.

"It doesn't compare to yours, though. Preacher man got you driving right."

"Thanks," she smiled.

He took out a manila envelope and handed it to her. "The young lady found in the trunk of the car is Claudia Reeves, a third-year law student at Atlanta University."

LaShaun sighed. "I figured that. I'd been holding out hope, but deep down I knew. She was one of my girls. Do you know who killed her?"

"Nothing is confirmed yet. I investigated Detective Victor Cruz like you told me, and he *is* a narc. But my informant says since his promotion to detective, he's had clean hands. He also said someone paid the head of a local gang two bricks to silence Claudia and the young man."

"Roderick Butler." She looked at photos of the crime scene. "How did you get these?"

"That's not important. I'm going to shake some more trees and see what else I can find out about Cruz. If he or Charlotte called the hit, I'll find out."

"Ok, thanks." She looked at a photo of a young girl in scrubs sitting in front of a condo smoking what appeared to be weed. "Who is this?"

"Word on the street is she knows something about the deacon's death. She's whom I'm meeting next, although she doesn't know it. Selling pills is her little side hustle, and my partner is setting up a little meet and greet."

"You think she knows anything?" LaShaun asked skeptically.

He nodded. "The streets don't lie. She knows *something*."

"What makes you think she'll talk?"

"They always talk."

"Is that why you have that scowl on your face? Trying to get into character?"

He winced. "Charlotte has transferred a considerable amount of cash from Sweet Dream's Accounts to her offshore accounts. I'm still tracking the money, but it looks like she's embezzling."

LaShaun nodded knowingly. "How much?"

"One point seven mil so far."

LaShaun clenched her teeth. "I felt like she was planning a coup or something. This just confirms it. You know I won't let her get away with it."

He caressed her face. "I know you won't. And when the time

is right, I can move it to another account for you. I'll contact you tomorrow with an update on weed girl."

She opened her car door. "Thanks for all your help. I really appreciate it."

He looked at her and smiled. Then, he pressed the car's *Push to Start* button. "I always got your back."

Chapter Twenty-Seven
COMMITTED SACRIFICE

Heiress knew she had to push aside her hurt feelings and continue her relationship with Vic as if nothing had changed. He was scheduled to get off work soon, and she'd cooked him a romantic dinner, but she was afraid her emotions would betray her.

When she thought about the late-night hookups, easy conversation, and freedom she felt when she was with him, she felt like a fool. And she wanted him to know it. She wanted him to experience the hurt she'd been feeling the past few days. But Karisma's future was on the line, so she vowed to keep her emotions under control.

At seven-thirty Vic arrived in a fitted knit cap, sweatshirt, and jeans. As he showered, Heiress plated the meal she'd prepared. When he finished, he came into the kitchen and snuggled her from behind as she poured two full glasses of wine. They swayed to the smooth jazz streaming through the speakers.

As one song ended and another began, Heiress gave Vic a long, sensual kiss that started at his mouth and ended at his chest. Her tongue traveled to his sensitive areas, forcing him to inhale before backing away. They wouldn't make it to the meal if Heiress continued.

Throughout dinner, the mood was light. However, Vic appeared to be distracted. He was saying the right things, but the lines that crept onto his face from time to time, indicated something was bothering him.

The more they appeared, the more her heartbeat quickened. She wondered whether he knew about the plan she'd concocted with her mom and LaShaun. Especially since he stared at her as she picked up the wine bottle to refill her glass.

"You sure you can handle that?" he asked. "I've never seen you drink so much."

Heiress placed the stem on the table, smiling seductively. "Maybe I want to be relaxed for whatever tonight brings."

Instead of playing along, Vic yawned. Her hurt feelings resurfaced.

"Are you kidding me right now?" She slid her hand down her body. "I'm offering you all this, and you're yawning on me!"

"I'm sorry, baby. Long day." He yawned again. "I've worked fourteen hours straight, and I'm exhausted. I'll make it up to you tomorrow."

"Are you sure that's all it is? Not your extracurricular activities?" she taunted.

Vic's face twisted in confusion. Heiress scowled right back at him.

"What's wrong? Have I done something that I'm not aware of?" he asked.

"Have you?" Heiress's aggressive tone matched her posture. She snatched her flute and gulped wine, then speared a piece of lettuce on her plate with a fork. They ate in silence until Vic took her hand in his.

"Talk to me. What's going on?"

She tried to calm herself so that she wouldn't blow her plan. "I'm sorry, babe. It's just that things aren't looking good for Karisma. I'm afraid the prosecution's case just might be strong enough for a conviction. All we have is her word, and we know how much a black person's word is to an all-white jury."

He straightened his back. "Jury selection hasn't begun. How do you know there's going to be an all-white jury? There could be more blacks than white. You never know."

"In your dreams," Heiress retorted. "The trial is taking place in a conservative county during an election year. Minorities make up twenty percent of the voters, and ninety-five percent of those won't be summoned. You do the math."

"That may be the case, but you shouldn't worry. Whites acquit blacks all the time."

"In this county? Name *one* case," Heiress challenged.

"I can't name them, but I'm sure they exist."

"Ok, I'll give you that. But even if there are more blacks on the jury, they still have a white judge from *Jaw-Ja*. And I've been in the courtroom when a good ole boy judge told my mom, *This is my courtroom. I don't care what the law is.* And he meant it."

He held up his hands in surrender. "Ok, babe, you win. I'm drained. Let's put these dishes away so I can lie down."

"Ok," Heiress answered deflated. "You can go to the bedroom, and I'll clean."

"You won't get an argument from me." He rose from the table and pecked her on the cheek, then walked slowly down the hall.

Later that night as they lay spooning, Heiress was drifting in and out of sleep, but Vic was restless. She reached over to her nightstand and turned on the lamp.

"What's wrong?" she asked.

"Nothing," he lied.

"Yes, there is. I can hear you thinking."

Vic sat up straight and scooted against the headboard. Heiress watched as he pulled his knees to his chest and laid his chin on them.

"Talk to me."

He remained quiet for several minutes, then straightened his legs so she could lie on his lap. "I want you to know I love you."

"You're scaring me. This is the first time you've said those words, but you sound like you're about to be sent to death row. What has you so down?" She grabbed his hands and held them.

He released her hand and caressed her head as he spoke.

"Three years ago, I helped my partner get rid of evidence against a very powerful person. I don't know what the evidence contained but doing what I did landed me a promotion to detective, with a considerable raise."

Heiress remained quiet.

"I know what I did was wrong, but I figured I wasn't hurting anyone. It wasn't a life-or-death case, so I swept it under the rug."

"Did anyone find out?"

"No. And a month or so later, I was tapped for a side gig. Again, nothing that hurt anyone. I would notify a certain person of impending investigations and give them time to fix things. Sometimes,

I investigated their clients and helped get charges dropped. Never anything to harm anyone else."

"Until now," Heiress blurted. She tried to catch it before it escaped, but she was too slow.

Victor's brows furrowed. "What do you mean, until now?"

Heiress had to think fast. "That's what I thought you were leading up to. That you'd never hurt anyone, until now." She carefully measured her words. "Am I wrong?"

Vic leaned against the headboard, staring at the ceiling. "I hope you don't hate me when I tell you this, but I'm involved in Karisma's case."

She bolted upright. "What do you mean involved?"

He rubbed his hands together and sighed. "I'm protecting Sweet Dreams Boutique and its owners."

"What do you mean, protecting?" Heiress tried not to appear panicked. "Stop talking in code and spit it out, Vic!"

"The specifics don't matter, Heiress. Karisma's innocent, and I feel horrible knowing that I'm helping the person who's framing her."

Heiress jumped up from the bed and grabbed her robe. "You knew that all this time and didn't tell me! Why would you do that? Are you using me for information?" she bellowed.

He rose from the bed and tried to hold her, but she shrugged him off.

"I'm sorry," he said convincingly. "In the beginning, yes. I was sent by Charlotte to find out how much you knew about LaShaun and Sweet Dreams. Then, one thing led to another, and I fell for you."

"When did you determine Karisma's innocence and why haven't you done anything about it? Why are you letting her get railroaded?"

Vic didn't respond. He got up and went over to the dorm-sized fridge Heiress had in the kitchenette and pulled out bottled water. He stared out the window as he sipped slowly.

"Why are you with me? The truth!" Heiress demanded.

"Because I'd rather be with you than anyone else." He turned to face her. "You have my heart."

"Does Charlotte know that?"

Vic hesitated before responding. "She knows we're involved, but she believes I'm keeping you close so I can be her eyes and ears."

"Are you?"

"You know I'm not."

"I don't know anything. What I thought I knew all these months turned out to be a lie," Heiress yelled.

She sat with her backside against her dresser, and Vic sat on the bench at the foot of her bed, facing her.

"I'm with you because I love you, Heiress. That's why this cover-up is eating me from the inside out."

"That's why?" Heiress's question dripped with sarcasm. "The fact that an innocent person is going to jail means nothing to you?"

"Of course, it does. I don't want to see Karisma go to jail."

"Then don't let her, Vic! Help us prove her innocence!"

Vic was stupefied. "Do you know what you're asking?"

"Look, you said you don't want to see Karisma in jail. Well, do the right thing. If you can't do it for yourself, do it for me," Heiress pleaded.

She knew she was asking a great deal from Vic, especially considering the danger of crossing Charlotte, but she wanted him to focus on what he'd be gaining instead of losing by doing the right thing.

So, she dropped her robe and stood in front of him, bringing his head to her breasts. He wrapped his arms around her waist. She knew, with the right motivation, he'd do the right thing. And she was just the motivation he needed.

Chapter Twenty-Eight
ALL RISE

The courtroom was nearing capacity when LaShaun arrived. Covid restrictions limited the gallery to witnesses and two members of the defendant's family - everyone else was forced to watch via a state-sanctioned streaming site.

As owners of Sweet Dreams Boutique, LaShaun and Charlotte were subpoenaed by the State prosecutor. She'd tried to subpoena their business records, but the judge denied the motion. During the trial, if the prosecutor could somehow introduce proof that the lingerie boutique was a prostitution ring, the judge would revisit his decision.

When LaShaun entered the courtroom, Kari and Kairo turned around, but quickly looked away. As their pastor, Langston was seated beside them. LaShaun chose a seat three rows back. She felt all eyes on her as she straightened her skirt and settled in. Then she felt a tap on her shoulder. She turned around and Liz was seated directly behind her, mouthing hello. LaShaun reciprocated.

Johnysa was talking to Karisma, who nodded here and there. Both women seemed calm and battle ready. Just as LaShaun picked up her purse to grab her pen and paper, the bailiff stepped forth and called the court to order.

"All rise," he directed. Once everyone stood, he announced, "The Superior Court for the State of Georgia, County of Cobb is now in session. The Honorable Judge Duncan Mathis presiding."

"Be seated," Judge Mathis ordered. Everyone complied without hesitancy. He went over housekeeping matters with Johnysa and the prosecutor, instructed everyone on how the court would proceed, and directed all witnesses to leave the courtroom. The morning was spent selecting the jury, and the prosecution presented their case after lunch.

LaShaun was not called to the stand that day, so she was clueless as to what occurred in the courtroom. She'd heard an officer guarding the witnesses say the jury was made up of eleven Whites, and one Black: nine women, three men, all over forty years of age, some nearing their late sixties.

A jury of her peers? LaShaun thought. *What a joke!*

From 8:30 a.m. to 5 p.m., LaShaun sat on a hard wooden bench, avoiding eye contact with Charlotte. They sat with each other for an hour during lunch but didn't engage in conversation about the trial. She knew Charlotte would attempt to violate that directive when the first opportunity presented itself.

At five o'clock, witnesses who hadn't been released were directed to return the next morning. LaShaun looked at Charlotte, and Charlotte returned her questioning stare with a shrug before they hightailed it out to the parking lot.

I know she's not following me, LaShaun thought as she noticed Charlotte's car tailing her on the drive home. When she entered her garage and threw her car in park, Charlotte had her hand on the door handle.

"Step back!" LaShaun scolded.

"Fine!" Charlotte stomped to the front door and waited.

"Why did you trail me home?" LaShaun asked as she put her key into the lock.

"So we can go over the testimony we're going to present at the trial."

LaShaun stared at her, stupefied. "We are barred from discussing the trial," she reminded her. "Besides, we can't prepare if we don't know what information they're seeking."

"But we can coordinate answers for everything we think we'll be asked," Charlotte countered.

"I'm not defying the judge's order." They entered the house.

Charlotte chuckled. "You can't keep your head buried in the sand like you always do, LaShaun. It's going to come back to bite you."

The women silently stood their ground, staring each other down with equal venom, until Charlotte shook her head in surrender. "Let me use the restroom, and I'll be on my way."

"Fine, but I'm serious. Don't ask me anything about the trial," LaShaun admonished.

Charlotte mumbled under her breath and threw her purse on the kitchen island, then hurried to the restroom. LaShaun poured herself a glass of water and took a banana from the counter. She viewed her mail until Charlotte returned.

"Alright," Charlotte said as she walked into the kitchen and placed a damp paper towel in the trash. "I'll touch base with you tomorrow, on the way to the courthouse. Get some rest."

LaShaun led her to the door. "I'm going to take a long hot bath and relax these aching muscles." They hugged when they reached the door and LaShaun watched as Charlotte got in her car and drove away.

When she turned around, Langston was behind her, and she screamed. "You scared the daylight out of me! Where did you come from?"

"I had work to do so I didn't go back to court after lunch. I was coming to meet you when you got here, but you weren't alone."

"Yeah, sorry about that. I had no idea Charlotte was going to follow me home." She rubbed the back of her neck in circular motions.

"I figured you'd be exhausted, so I ordered us something for dinner. I hope you don't mind."

LaShaun smiled gratefully. Langston was hurting, but he was still compassionate. "Not at all. I'm grateful you did. Do I have time to shower?"

Langston looked like a wounded pup, wanting to run into the arms of the owner that harmed him, yet staying at bay. "Take all the time you need. I scheduled delivery for an hour from now."

LaShaun felt horrible. She knew she caused damage to their marriage and him, but she also knew they could work it out if they didn't lose faith in each other. She touched his arm as she moved past him. "Thank you," she whispered.

"I'll let you know when the food arrives," he replied.

Forty-five minutes later, they were eating dinner and watching highlights from the trial. According to the online anchorman and the guest attorney he was interviewing, the prosecutor presented a compelling case against Karisma, and in the next two days, her presentation to the jury would end.

The anchorman concluded his coverage with, "Before the

prosecution rests tomorrow, we expect she will call LaShaun Delaney and Charlotte Montgomery to the stand. Stay tuned as we search for the truth and answer the question everyone's asking, 'Will the owners of Sweet Dreams Boutique take the stand, and if they do, will they plead the fifth?"

Langston's eye twitched, and LaShaun closed her eyes. It was going to be a long night.

Chapter Twenty-Nine
UNHINGED

The next morning, the judge had to tend to an emergency, and court was postponed until one o'clock. After receiving the cold shoulder from Langston all night, LaShaun didn't want to stay home, so she made the long drive to Charlotte's cabin. She was surprised to find Charlotte waiting for her on the porch when she arrived.

LaShaun walked up the steps, into Charlotte's open arms, then followed her inside the house to the living room. Charlotte's assistant took LaShaun's purse to the guest bedroom, while the butler handed her a glass of iced tea and Charlotte bottled water. Then they sauntered over to the couch and sat facing each other.

"What have you been doing this morning?" LaShaun asked. She knew what Charlotte had been doing because Monster cloned her computer and monitored her online activity. She'd spoken with him on the way to the cabin, and he'd informed her Charlotte was making big moves to take over the Boutique.

"Shredding documents and proofing our new website."

"Why? What's wrong with the one we've been using all this time?" LaShaun drank her tea.

"We have no idea what the trial will uncover, so I've taken matters into my own hands. We're now operating our main business on the dark web."

She thinks she's so slick. "When were you going to tell me?" LaShaun pretended to be more upset than she was. Monster had assured her he could reverse anything Charlotte did. For the past two weeks, he'd been working with Johnysa and Heiress, helping to secure Karisma's freedom and save the Boutique.

"You have so much on your plate I didn't want to bother you. But it's not going to affect how you handle the financial side of things. Are you ready for tomorrow?"

"Don't change the subject. I'm tired of you hiding things from me." She took another sip of her tea.

"I'm not *hiding* anything. I'm taking care of business as I've always done. Why are you behaving like I'm doing something underhanded?" Her neck turned red, and the color was slowly traveling to her face.

LaShaun decided to dial it back. "I'm sorry, Char. This trial has me on edge." She drank more tea. "This tea is calming, though. What kind is it?"

"You don't need to worry about the trial. I have it all under control."

"How? The judge is beyond reproach, and the jury is sequestered."

"I have Victor on it. Everything will be over soon."

"From your lips to God's ears," LaShaun responded.

Charlotte's eyes filled with rage. "Forget God! You're here because I do what I do!"

"The devil is a lie! Doing what you do got us into this m--!"

"Doing what I do will set Karisma free, keep Sweet Dreams Boutique running smoothly, and allow you to continue living a fairy tale!" Charlotte cut LaShaun off with veins bulging from her neck.

LaShaun tried to push out a response, but her tongue felt thick, and words were lodged in her throat. Alarmed, she tried lifting her arms, but each felt like it weighed twenty pounds. She could hear and see, so she tried to signal with her eyes something was terribly wrong.

"Don't fight it," Charlotte said calmly. "This is for your good, and you'll thank me when it's over." LaShaun blinked in response, a tear trickling down her cheek.

Charlotte pulled a tissue from the small box on her side table and dabbed it. "We don't know what's in store for us this afternoon or tomorrow, so I have a plan that will take us away from Atlanta. I'm going to protect you."

LaShaun grunted as loud as she could, trying to alert Charlotte's assistant and butler that something was amiss.

"Stop that!" Charlotte yelled. "No one is coming to your rescue. We are leaving, and all of this will be behind us."

LaShaun fought to keep her eyes open.

"Don't worry about Langston," Charlotte hissed. "Your relationship is hanging on by a thread anyway. After a year in our new home, you'll forget he ever existed."

With tremendous effort, LaShaun shook her head no.

"Langston doesn't love you anymore!" Charlotte roared. "Hasn't he shown that to you!"

When LaShaun closed her eyes, Charlotte lifted one of her arms and released it. As it fell, the weight of it pulled LaShaun's torso to the left.

"Oops," Charlotte said as she straightened her. "I'll take care of you now. We will live happily ever after."

As Charlotte stroked LaShaun's hair like a baby, a bell chimed, waking LaShaun. Charlotte looked at her phone. "Ahh, here's Vic now." Moments later she opened the door, and Vic entered.

"What took you so long? I've been waiting for hours," she asked gruffly.

"I had some loose ends to tie up." He looked at LaShaun, who shrieked.

He attempted to move in her direction, but Charlotte grabbed him by the forearm. "Don't worry about her. She's fine. I gave her something to numb her body until today's hearing is over. It'll wear off in a few hours."

Victor stroked his chin. "I don't understand. Is that necessary?"

Charlotte waved him off. "Don't worry about it. Is everything going as planned with the jurors?"

"Better than planned," he answered. "We have enough jurors to force a mistrial."

"And you're sure they're onboard?" she questioned.

"Well, they'll receive a handsome payday if they vote *not guilty*, and a deep grave if they don't."

Charlotte curled her lips into an evil sneer. "That's what I like to hear. I knew I can count on you."

She led Victor to the kitchen. She sat at the table and crossed her legs as he stood near the island. "Bring me up to date," she directed.

"Well...as you requested, I doctored Rod's rideshare report to show he dropped Claudia at LaShaun's address the morning after she left the hotel," he gleefully reported. "His local manager will take the stand and verify that this afternoon."

"What about the video?" Charlotte inquired.

"I mailed it to the prosecutor. The guy you hired did a fantastic job replacing you with LaShaun. It shows her entering an abandoned warehouse and returning to her car shortly after two gunshots are heard. Moments later, several men bring out two dead bodies and put them in the trunk of a car. Then, LaShaun drives away."

Claudia screeched and clapped her hands in delight. "Good job," she cackled loudly.

Vic didn't respond to her compliment or theatrics. "I also hid Claudia's trench coat and Rod's ID at her home, so that should give the detectives enough probable cause to obtain a warrant for her arrest."

Charlotte had a dazed look in her eyes. "Soon I'll be the sole owner of Sweet Dreams Boutique and LaShaun will be dependent on me for everything!"

Vic glanced at LaShaun. She had fallen asleep again. "I'm still puzzled by your decision to frame her for the murders of the deacon, Rod, *and* Claudia. You've told me many times she means more to you than your own family. Why have you turned against her?"

"I'll never turn against her. I would give my life for her, but she'd rather play *first lady* to Langston. Now that he has shown his true colors, we can leave and set up shop elsewhere, and the two of us can live happily ever after. I'll make sure she never sees the inside of a jail cell if she agrees to come with me. I'm the only one who can love her like she needs to be loved."

"But you can't force her to love you. She'll resent you."

"No, she won't! Shut up!" Charlotte screamed.

Vic immediately held out his hands and pumped them up and down. "Hey, calm down. I'm on your side," he coaxed.

Charlotte rose from her chair and placed her hands on his arms, rubbing them. "I'm sorry for that outburst. I just don't like my loyalty questioned."

"It's okay. I get it."

"Thank you for being such a great friend, and always coming when I call. Would you like some tea?"

"No, I'm good," Vic replied. "I'm going to leave now...but I'll see you in court later today."

Charlotte followed him to the door. As he placed his hand on the doorknob, she injected him with the same serum she'd put in LaShaun's tea. He fell to the floor with a thud.

She immediately summoned her butler, and they pulled him to the sofa and handcuff his hand to LaShaun's foot. Then, they handcuffed his foot to an end table. Minutes later, he was asleep.

The next morning, LaShaun woke with an acrid taste in her mouth. The butler entered the living room a short time later and removed her cuffs. Victor was still on the floor, asleep and handcuffed to the table. She rolled her neck and stretched her back as the butler led her to the restroom. He stood with a gun pointed at her as she released waste. Neither of them said a word.

When she returned to the living room, Victor was still in the same spot. The butler handcuffed her hands and feet. Then, he nudged Victor with his foot until he regained consciousness. Victor groaned as he attempted to lift his body from the floor.

Although his hands were free, Victor was in too much pain to tackle the butler. He winced and grabbed his shoulder as the butler released the cuffs from his feet and lifted him from the floor. It was then he noticed Charlotte's assistant with a gun aimed in their direction.

Victor went to the restroom and returned without incident. His hands and feet were cuffed, and he was placed on the sofa, next to LaShaun. Then the butler and assistant left them alone.

"What time is it?" Victor whispered.

"I don't know, but the sun is coming up, so it's early morning."

Vic tried loosening the cuffs but couldn't. LaShaun saw his fruitless efforts and said, " We're trapped like animals, and there's nothing we can do to save ourselves. If I could talk to Charlotte, maybe I can convince her that I want to go with her."

"Go where?" Vic asked.

"I'm not sure. Somewhere the authorities can't reach her and extradite her to this country, I'm sure."

"She can only travel about 400 miles in a helicopter."

"Yes, but her pilot takes her to an airport in Tennessee, where she boards her private plane."

"We can't allow her to make it to her plane. The authorities should be at her home as we speak, and soon they'll be here and looking for her."

Chapter Thirty
THE FINAL SAY

Karisma waited patiently as the judge signed bench warrants for LaShaun and Charlotte. They failed to show up for court, and he was permitting their arrest. Yesterday, he granted a continuance to give the prosecutor time to locate them, but she was unable to do so. Now, with no other witnesses to question, she had no choice but to rest her case.

Johnysa's first witness was Nurse Adrianna Pennington. Due to Monster's not-so-subtle encouragement, she agreed to appear in court and testify against Charlotte. She was sworn in and took her seat on the witness stand. After running through her credentials and overcoming the prosecutor's numerous objections, Adrianna's testimony began.

"Mrs. Pennington, were you on the schedule at County Memorial Hospital on December 27, 2019?" Johnysa asked.

"Yes," Adrianna spoke into the microphone.

"And what time did you work on that date?"

"We were short staffed, so I arrived at 7 a.m., and left at 11:15."

Johnysa strolled to the jury box and stood. "And on that day, did you have an opportunity to speak with a person named Charlotte Montgomery?"

"Yes."

The prosecutor jumped to her feet. "Objection, Your Honor. Relevancy."

"Overruled," Judge Peale ordered before Johnysa could say anything. Then he looked to Johnysa. "Make it plain or the testimony will be stricken from the record."

Johnysa had to tread lightly. During pre-trial motions, the judge ruled opposing counsel could not introduce her sex trade theory to the jury without evidence to prove it. Johnysa didn't want to be the one to open the door and pave the way for her to question Adrianna about it.

"Please tell the court the nature of your conversation."

Adrianna cleared her throat and scanned the courtroom. There was no one in the gallery but Karisma's parents and the deacon's family. She leaned forward and spoke.

"Ummm...Charlotte...I mean Ms. Montgomery, asked me to give a patient some medicine." Adrianna's voice trailed off.

"Please speak into the microphone so that the court reporter can accurately record your response," Johnysa directed. She'd heard the answer but wanted it repeated for effect.

"Ms. Montgomery asked me to give a patient some medicine."

"And do you recall the patient's name?"

"Yes, it was Archibald Thomas."

"And were you Archibald Thomas's nurse on December 27th?"

"No," Adrianna said as she rubbed the hem of her jacket between her thumb and index finger.

"Did she tell you what she wanted you to give Mr. Thomas?"

Adrianna looked down at her hands but didn't speak.

"Please answer the question, Ms. Pennington."

The witness cleared her throat. "She wanted me to give him something that would make him sleep...forever."

"Objection!" The prosecution yelled as she jumped to her feet. "Motion to strike. This is the first time I'm hearing anything of the sort."

Johnysa countered. "Your Honor, Ms. Pennington and the nature of her testimony only recently came to my attention. I notified DA Muhammad immediately. She had all day yesterday to speak with her but chose not to do so."

"Overruled," the judge stated.

"And by sleep forever," Johnysa peered at the jurors, "what do you mean?

"She wanted me to kill him with a lethal dose of Morphine," Adrianna confirmed. The jurors took notes on their writing pads. They paid more attention to her testimony than any the entire trial. Adrianna's testimony was pure entertainment.

"And did you give Mr. Thomas a lethal dose of medication?"

"No ma'am, I did not."

"Did you have a conversation with Ms. Montgomery any time thereafter?"

"No."

"Did you enter his hospital room at any time?"

"No."

"On any day?"

"No," Adrianna stressed as firmly as she had the other two times.

"Now you indicated Ms. Montgomery approached you. Did anyone else approach you about harming Mr. Thomas?"

"No."

"And did you ever see anyone harm Mr. Thomas?"

"No."

"And did you harm Mr. Thomas?"

"No."

"Thank you, Ms. Pennington." She turned to the prosecutor, "Your witness."

The prosecutor stood in front of her table. "Ms. Pennington, you didn't contact the authorities and let them know about Ms. Montgomery, isn't that true?"

"Yes."

"And you didn't notify my office that Ms. Montgomery had made such a request, true?"

"Yes."

"This is the first time you've shared this information with anyone investigating this case, isn't that right."

"Yes, but I'm telling the truth," she answered.

"It's mighty convenient you waited until now to tell it, isn't it?"

Johnysa sprouted from her seat. "Objection, Your honor. Argumentative."

"I withdraw the question, Your Honor." She took her time walking to her seat. Johnysa glared at her until she sat down."

"Redirect?" The judge asked Johnysa.

"No," Your Honor.

"I'm going to allow a brief recess so the jurors can stretch their legs. Court will resume in fifteen minutes," the judge announced.

Late yesterday evening, after weeks of trying, Jorge managed to hack into the hospital's database. He retrieved security footage from

December 27th. Said footage had been deleted from the hospital's hard drive, but he was able to pull it from the cloud.

During the recess, she showed the video to the prosecutor, who agreed to allow it to be admitted into evidence without objection.

When court resumed, Johnysa called Detective Wyndall Williams to the stand. After laying the proper foundation, she got to the meat of the officer's testimony.

"Drawing your attention to the video we just viewed, were you able to identify the person entering the hospital at 6:45 p.m. on December 27th and leaving the same hospital at 7:10 p.m.?"

"Yes," the detective answered.

"And how did you ascertain that information?" Johnysa asked.

"A security camera captured the vehicle's license plate as she pulled out of the parking lot and drove away from the hospital. We were able to run the vehicle registration."

"And can you tell the jury who owned the vehicle?"

"It was owned by Success Commodities Unlimited, a corporation registered in Morocco."

"And what did you do with that information, detective?"

"We contacted the Federal Bureau of Investigation, and they informed us the corporation was owned by Charlotte Montgomery.".

The jury shifted in their seats, and the prosecutor did not object to the hearsay evidence being presented. The evidence helped the State as much as it did Karisma. Since there was no objection, the judge allowed it to remain in the record.

"Were you able to determine whom she visited at the hospital, detective?"

"Yes. We scanned the video surveillance archives and saw her entering the room of Mr. Archibald Thomas at 6:52 pm." The jurors gasped.

"And what did you do after ascertaining this information?"

"We obtained a warrant to search Ms. Montgomery's home, and at eight o'clock this morning, officers retrieved a trench coat that appeared to be the one Ms. Claudia Reeves was seen wearing when she left the Lancaster Hotel on the night of December 19th. We also retrieved a copy of Roderick Butler's rideshare identification card in a barbecue grill, partially burned."

"And what did you do with those items, if anything?" She glanced at the jurors.

He leaned closer to the mic. "Well, we searched the pockets of the trench coat and found a small syringe. We were able to lift a fingerprint from it."

"Is anything significant about the syringe?"

"Yes. Mr. Archibald was killed by a lethal injection of Morphine. It's our theory it was injected into his IV. So, we're sending the syringe to the lab for testing."

"And if it comes back possible for Morphine?"

"Then that's additional probable cause to arrest Ms. Montgomery for the death of Mr. Archibald Thomas, Robert Butler, and Claudia Reeves."

Johnysa let that sink in before asking her next question.

"Now, you said *additional* probable cause. Can you tell the jury what you mean by that?"

"Forensics were able to lift fingerprints from Mr. Butler's ID, and they belong to Ms. Charlotte Montgomery. They also located several additional items in the home, one of which was a black dress. We believe that to be the dress *Ms. Claudia Reeves* was wearing at the hotel the night *she* was with Ms. Archibald Thomas. We were able to pull hair from the dress to test for DNA."

Karisma's parents had been silent the entire trial, but they couldn't control themselves any longer. Her mother yelled, "Thank you!" Her father clapped his hands and pumped his right fist up and down in victory.

The judge eventually restored order to the courtroom, but not before they expressed their jubilation. When he allowed Johnysa to continue, she had a follow-up question.

"To clarify, detective. Are you saying that Ms. Karisma Stanley was not at the hotel with Mr. Archibald Thomas on December 19, 2019?"

"That's correct."

"And are you also saying Ms. Karisma Stanley was not seen on video surveillance leaving Mr. Thomas's room or the hospital on December 27, 2019?"

"That's correct." He looked at Karisma and nodded, then smiled at the jury.

"No further questions," Johnysa announced.

The judge directed the prosecutor to proceed with cross-examination."

The prosecutor pushed her chair back and stood. "Your Honor, the State has obtained evidence sufficient to show that someone other than Ms. Karisma Stanley likely killed Mr. Archibald Thomas, and believing it to be in the best interest of the State of Georgia, we'd like to dismiss all charges against Ms. Stanley, with our apologies."

"Alright, if that's the State's position, the charges against the defendant, Ms. Karisma Stanley, are hereby dismissed." Then he looked towards Karisma. "Ms. Stanley, it's my pleasure to say you're free to go."

Karisma didn't hear Johnysa congratulating her or Deyja telling her it was time to go home. As soon as the judge said she was free to go, she placed her head on the table and cried repeatedly, "Thank you, God." She'd been bound so long she'd forgotten what freedom felt like. Now, there was a lightness to her spirit she wanted to last an eternity. And she didn't get it from cutting herself.

When Karisma stopped giving Him praise, she rose from her chair and hugged her parents. Between laughter and tears, they walked out of the courtroom and exited the courthouse through a side entrance, to avoid the media.

When her parents thanked Johnysa, she declared, "It's not my doing. The Lord always has the final say!"

Chapter Thirty-One
DELIVERANCE

Charlotte was awakened before sunrise by an alarm indicating her home in the city had an intruder. As she jumped from her bed to review the security monitor, she saw police in riot gear use a battering ram to gain entry through the front door. Frantic, she contacted the judge who denied the search warrant a few months back, but he didn't answer. Neither did any of her contacts in the Sheriff's department. So, she was forced to watch for hours as officers entered and exited her home, removing boxes she'd stashed behind a hidden wall.

"Ugghhhh!" she yelled at the top of her lungs. She ran to her bedroom and removed her gun from the safe, then hurried to the living room. "Which one of you betrayed me?" she yelled. She pointed the gun back and forth, between the two.

"What are you talking about?" Vic hollered. "Put the gun down." She walked over to him and placed the gun to his head.

"Was it you?" she asked calmly.

"No! I would never do that. You know I'll ride with you until the wheels fall off!" he lied as he tried to move his head away from the weapon. She stared at LaShaun and aimed the gun at her heart.

"Then it was you," she said as tears streamed down her face. In a childlike voice, she asked, "Why would you do it? You know I love you."

"I love you, too," LaShaun said. "I didn't betray you, and neither did Vic. We both have your back. Maybe the police found something on their own."

Charlotte eyed LaShaun suspiciously. "I'm no fool! One of you is lying, and if you don't come clean, I'm putting a bullet in both of you."

"Why would we betray you?" LaShaun asked shakily. "We have just as much to lose as you." As she spoke, she spied Monster peeking down the stairs. He put his finger to his mouth, telling her not to make a sound.

Charlotte called her butler, but he didn't come.

"May I use the restroom? Then we all can fly away from here. Go someplace they'll never find us," LaShaun tried to convince her.

"Yes, if they got evidence on you, they got it on us," Vic added.

She looked at LaShaun and swatted the tears away. "I know you're trying to get released so you can try to catch me off guard, but it won't work. Even if you get away from me, you won't be able to leave the property. My men will kill you the moment you step foot on the porch, and no one will ever find you or Vic."

She called the butler again, and there was still no answer. She cursed, and then directed LaShaun to get up.

"I can't with these cuffs on my hands and feet. Can you take them off?" She asked feigning innocence.

Charlotte chuckled. "Nice try. Get up the best way you can." She kept the gun aimed in her direction.

LaShaun tried not to look in Monster's direction. She scooted her butt to the edge of the sofa, then clumsily stood.

"Now don't try anything funny. I *will* shoot you," Charlotte warned. She had the gun aimed at her, then stepped back. "Walk."

LaShaun hobbled slowly passed the coffee table that was a couple of feet from the sofa. She shuffled down the long highway to the bathroom before finally reaching the bathroom door and holding her wrists out.

"No, you're going to stay cuffed. I'll help you get your pants down."

LaShaun rolled her eyes and turned towards the door. Charlotte stepped to the side and opened it. LaShaun entered.

After she used the restroom, Charlotte awkwardly pulled LaShaun's pants to her waist. Then she followed as LaShaun made her way toward the living room.

When they passed the kitchen, and LaShaun pivoted her body towards the living room, Monster ran from behind the island and tackled Charlotte before she had an opportunity to react. Her gun flew from her hand, and LaShaun lost her footing, falling violently to the floor.

As Charlotte struggled to get away, Monster pinned a knee in her back and held a gun to her head. "Don't move!" he growled.

"Are you okay?" Vic asked LaShaun. He had moved to the edge of the sofa.

"I'm a little shaken, but I'll live," she said excitedly. She looked at Monster and mouthed, *Thank you.*

"You don't know whom you're messing with," Charlotte said as she writhed beneath him. "You're a dead man!"

"Who's gonna kill me?" Monster asked. "The five men I killed outside or the three I killed moments ago?"

Charlotte didn't respond.

Monster took the key to the handcuffs from Charlotte's jacket pocket and released Vic's handcuffs. Vic then uncuffed his feet and got on his knees to free LaShaun.

Out of nowhere, the butler entered the room and fired a round at Monster. The bullet hit the coffee table and ricocheted, hitting LaShaun in her left side as she raised her torso.

The second shot caught Monster, in his shoulder, knocking him forward. He was able to tuck and roll to a position where he had a clear shot at the butler. He fired his semi-automatic weapon, killing the butler instantly.

As Charlotte scrambled to get her weapon, Vic managed to knock her over. Then a thundering sound came from the direction of the front and side door as swat entered with weapons drawn.

"Drop your weapon and get down on the floor," one of them yelled. Monster and Vic did as they were told and LaShaun passed out from loss of blood.

EPILOGUE

LaShaun woke the next day with Langston holding her hands and praying. As she attempted to squeeze his hand, he lifted his head.

"Oh, thank God," he declared. "Let me get the doctor."

It was déjà vu and LaShaun couldn't tell if the last few months had been a dream or reality. When the doctor entered the room, he smiled and approached her bedside.

"Hello, I'm Dr. Bracken. You were rushed here by medevac following a gunshot wound. We performed surgery to remove the bullet from your left side. Luckily, we were able to get it, and you should make a full recovery."

The tubes traveling down LaShaun's throat prevented her from speaking, but she nodded in understanding.

"Thank you so much Doc, Langston exclaimed. You are a blessing."

Dr. Bracken gave Langston additional instructions and left the room. Langston stood beside LaShaun and caressed her head.

After thanking God for saving her life, he held her hands and caressed them. She made grunting noises and questioned him with her eyes. After several guesses at what she was trying to convey, he finally asked, "Do you want to know what happened to Charlotte?"

She nodded her head.

"She's in custody. I'm not sure about everything they charged her with, but she'll probably be gone for a long time. I don't know what impact her case is going to have on you, but we'll cross that bridge when we get to it. For now, we'll just focus on you getting better."

Two days later, she was well enough to go home. As Langston went downstairs to get the car and she was being discharged, the nurse handed her an envelope. It contained a get-well card from Monster. It included a handwritten note.

Shaun, I know that you love Langston, and we can never get back what we once had. But I want you to know that I will always love you. When you're ready, please contact me. I found some information on Charlotte's computer that might interest you. It's regarding your daughter. For now, focus on getting well. I'm always a phone call away, and I always have your back. Forever yours, Monster.

A week later, as LaShaun lay in bed thinking about all the mistakes she'd made, she couldn't help but thank God for his grace and mercy. She'd given Him her hand while she lay in her hospital bed, and she was determined to live a life pleasing to Him.

Langston had taken time away from DMI and was providing round-the-clock care. They hadn't addressed their problems, but they were more than cordial to each other, and the love between them still flowed. She had no doubt they would grow old together.

She was flipping through the channels trying to find a cooking show when the doorbell rang. Soon thereafter, Johnysa and Heiress entered her bedroom. They'd brought lunch for her, Langston, and Rosa.

They gave her hugs as Langston placed two chairs from the kitchen beside the bed. He then put a bed tray across LaShaun's lap, laid her food on it, and left the room.

As LaShaun ate Broccoli and Cheese soup, Johnysa told her all about the trial and reported that Karisma was doing well. Thankfully, she already had a therapist and was able to begin her sessions quickly. She would return to AU the following semester.

"On another note, I ended things with Vic," Heiress announced sadly.

"I'm sorry, honey. I know you cared for him," LaShaun said lovingly. She reached out her hand and Heiress grabbed it.

"I'm happy he told the police everything he knew about Charlotte and admitted you had nothing to do with the killings, but I could never feel safe around him."

"He's a good guy who got caught in Charlotte's web," Johnysa added. "He'll spend a few years behind bars but, with the information he provided the district attorney and us, the authorities will shave years off his sentence. We couldn't have won an acquittal without him."

"What do you think will happen to Charlotte?" LaShaun asked.

Heiress and Johnysa looked at each other as if withholding a secret.

"We're going to leave and let you rest," Johnysa said as she and Heiress grabbed their purses. "We'll talk about Charlotte another day."

"No, sit back down." LaShaun pointed to the chairs they'd been sitting on. "You're hiding something. What is it?"

Heiress and Johnysa looked at each other. "You might as well tell her mom. She's going to find out anyway."

Fearing the worst, LaShaun steepled her hands and pleaded, "Tell me what happened."

Against her better judgment, Johnysa gave her the latest development.

"On the way to her arraignment, the guards escorting her were ambushed, and Charlotte was able to escape. Police are still trying to find her, but they believe she has already fled the country."

LaShaun closed her eyes and took a deep breath.

"Say something," Johnysa encouraged.

LaShaun looked at her with fire in her eyes.

"I thought my nightmare was over, but with Charlotte on the run...it's just beginning!"